CANNON'S MOUTH

A RAFFERTY P.I. NOVEL
BOOK 5

BILL DUNCAN

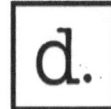

d squared
publishing.

THE RAFFERTY P.I. SERIES

Rafferty's Rules

Last Seen Alive

Poor Dead Cricket

Wrong Place, Wrong Time

Cannon's Mouth

Fatal Sisters

False Gods

Wright & Wrong

Down The Barrel

———

Scan the QR code below for more details and
the up-to-date list of all books in the series.

Cannon's Mouth

First published in the United States in 1990 by Ballantine Books, a division of Random House, Inc., New York, and simultaneously in Canada by Random House of Canada Limited, Toronto.

This version published in 2017 by d squared publishing.

Cover design by d squared publishing

Ebook ISBN: 978-0-6480370-8-8

P'back ISBN: 978-0-6453283-7-0

For enquiries regarding this book, please email: bill@duncanandlee.com

PROLOGUE

Excerpt - COMBAT ACTION MAGAZINE, pg 79

1

t was stinking hot in Dallas the week I followed a tobacco and candy delivery truck around town. The truck driver was a guy named Bartelles. He was either crooked or a born loser.

"Goddamnedest thing you ever saw," Shanahan had growled. "Three times so far, and he's due again, I'm telling you. Any day now that son of a bitch is gonna come in here with some song and dance about how he was mugged, or kids swiped product from the truck, or a pickpocket must have lifted the big wallet with the company cash. It'll be bullshit, every word of it, but if I fire him, I'll be up to my ass in union troubles. Unless I can prove he's shitting me." Shanahan leered at me over his Manager—Transport desk sign. "Go prove Bartelles is shitting me."

I quoted Shanahan a flat price for a week-long tail, with a bonus for hard evidence. By three o'clock on the Tuesday afternoon I knew I'd screwed up. There should have been another zero on the end of that weekly rate.

We were downtown then, Bartelles and I, deep in the broiling bowels of the inner city. The sun was still high. And hot. There was no breeze. Rush hour loomed large on the automotive horizon. The Mustang's air-conditioner was broken again. I had a soggy shirt-back, a knifing headache, and a helluva thirst, but nothing on Bartelles.

It was the kind of day they should videotape in living color and Sweat-O-Vision, and show it to anyone tempted to answer one of those BE A PRIVATE INVESTIGATOR! ads.

And what the day lacked in comfort, it more than made up for in boring. So far I'd watched Bartelles lug cartons of smokes and candy bars into maybe fifty grocery stores and newsstands and bars and bowling alleys and … you name it, we stopped there. The damnedest thing was, Bartelles was doing all the work, not me, but the heat didn't seem to bother him. He was a short, jaunty guy who trotted everywhere.

Just one more day of this, I decided, or another three degrees. Either one, and I could learn to hate this guy.

On the fifty-first, or maybe it was the eighty-first, stop, I slipped into a loading zone half a block back from the parked tobacco truck. Up ahead bouncy little Bartelles rattled up the truck's roller door and grabbed another box. He walked toward a hotel service entrance, moving first through a shimmer of heat haze, then out of sight. *Abracadabra! And for my next trick …*

I leaned forward slowly; my shirt came away from the vinyl seat-back with that slimy, cool pull that feels like it should make a loud noise. I creaked and grunted and levered myself out of the Mustang and trudged across the sidewalk to a postage stamp-size park wedged between two buildings.

Good move, Rafferty. A light breeze somehow meandered through the surrounding buildings and drifted through a shadow just my size. It was a good ten degrees cooler than the Mustang. Ahh, bliss.

I was not alone in the little oasis. There was also a man in a short-sleeved white shirt. He stayed out in the sun, the dummy, where he paced around in tight circles and glanced warily at me every five or six seconds. He had a rolled-up magazine in one hand. He alternated whacking the magazine against his leg and waving it around like he wanted me to notice it. Or notice him. He smiled at me. It was a nervous, hopeful smile.

I do not need this, I thought. Of all the things I definitely do not need, this is a biggie.

The man paced. I ignored him. I thought about cold beer and dinner that night with Hilda Gardner and how wonderful she looked whenever she—

"Great magazine, huh?" The man finally stopped pacing. He stood a careful six feet from me and held up his magazine like a talisman. Or a shield. It was one of those quasi-military magazines. They're aimed at ex-soldiers, I guess, but I've always wondered how many of their readers are wannabees, guys who think they, too, could be a gen-u-ine hairy-chested mercenary soldier if only they could figure out which end of the gun goes *bang*.

"What do you think?" the man said. "Good ads, right? I think so." He was forty-five, give or take, with a comfortable roll of fat around his middle and pale indoor-worker skin. He had thinning dark hair and a round chin. His hands shook; the magazine fluttered. He was sweating as much as I was, but I thought he had a different reason.

I glared at him. Okay, so it wasn't my very best glare. I was tired and hot; it had already been a long day.

"Look, I'm sorry I'm late," he said. His voice rose sharply at the end; he caught it, swallowed and started again. "I'm sorry. I was … detained. I'm not used to this."

"How are you on busted noses?" I said. Talking to him was a mistake, I knew that, but I figured if I came on strong, he'd get the idea and take a hike. Then it suddenly occurred to me that he might grin and offer me money to beat him up. Uh-oh.

Neither of those things happened.

"Good," he said. "You were right. In your ad, I mean. Aggressive. And look, never mind what I said; it's all right about the price. I'll pay it. I'm here, aren't I?" His face clouded briefly, and he said, "You're sure there won't be any problems? I mean, for that much money, there shouldn't be, but …"

Down the block the delivery truck wavered in the heat. There was no sign of Bartelles.

"No problems," I said to the nervous man. I reached across my chest to peel the clammy shirt away from my left side. He jumped back a half step, then seemed to realize I wasn't practicing my quick-draw technique. He sighed and came a little closer.

He dropped his voice to a hoarse whisper. "Okay, then. Thursday night. The day after tomorrow, if that's all right with you. Make it look like a robbery. He'll be alone. And for goodness sake, don't do it if there are customers in the—oh, yeah, you wouldn't want any witnesses, would you?"

I shook my head slowly and scowled. That felt good; the guy winced a little. Okay, the glare is out; the scowl is definitely in. I felt vaguely disassociated and tried to remember when I had last had anything to drink.

The man shuddered and turned his head away. "I just wish there was another way," he said. "But like I said on the phone, I can't think of anything. It's gone too far. We're about to go under. Without the cash from the keyman policy, I—" He braced himself and said harshly, "Just do it, all right? Do it."

Then he turned and slowly walked in a circle until he was

back where he'd started, facing me. "Only, uh, can you do it without hurting him? Well, I know killing him is … but … do you know what I mean?"

I showed him another scowl.

He sighed. "All right," he said; then, "Oh, I almost forgot." He reached into his shirt pocket, tugged at something, couldn't get it free, dropped the magazine, picked up the magazine, and finally came up with a three-by-five index card. He handed it to me. His hand shook quite a bit now.

The card had an address written in pencil and a brief description of someone. *Five nine, balding, long ears, bushy eyebrows.*

"I wrote down what Max looks like," the man said. "So you wouldn't make a mistake." Then he seemed to think about that and blurted, "Not *mistake!* I didn't mean *mistake.* I just meant so … so you'd be … um, to help! I wrote it down to help you, that's all."

I scowled a third time. Hey, if something works, I stick with it. To go with the scowl, I tried for a voice somewhere between Jack Palance and Lee Marvin. "How do I reach you?" I said. My voice came out at least four tones too high; more like Jack Lemmon and Lee Remick.

"At the same number," he said. "At least until Thursday morning. Uh, should we go now? Before someone sees us together?"

Oh, damn. Down the block Bartelles had returned. He was closing the truck door.

"Well, yeah, but …"

Bartelles sauntered around the truck and hopped into the cab. Why right now, for god's sake?

"I'll leave first," the nervous man said. He peered around the corner, then scurried away. He kept close to the buildings and darted rapid glances over his shoulder every five or six steps. He blended in with the other pedestrians about like Dolly Parton in the Cowboys' locker room.

But let's face it, I wasn't exactly Mr. Cool myself. I followed the man for a few steps, then stood in the middle of the sidewalk with my head flopping back and forth. I didn't know whether to stick with the man who wanted Max murdered or continue my tail on Bartelles.

Down the block, the truck wheeled into traffic with a blurt of diesel smoke.

In the other direction the nervous man scuttled around the corner.

Make up your mind, Rafferty.

Well, hell, I didn't know who the nervous man was, but I knew where and when the hit was supposed to be. Whoever Max was, he'd be okay until Thursday night. The cops could take it from here.

Besides, I had a lot of sweat invested in the tobacco caper.

So I followed Bartelles.

When I screw up, I screw up big.

2

Two cigarette deliveries later, Bartelles began to work his way out of the central business district. Way to go! We were going to beat the rush hour. Bartelles might be crooked, I decided, but he was no dummy.

We went up McKinney toward Lemmon. When we went past Gardner's Antiques, I looked for Hilda. Too much sun glare; I couldn't see anything through the shop windows.

The air coming through the Mustang's lowered windows was warm and soupy, but it moved and that was a big improvement. So was a quart of orange juice I bought at a mom-and-pop grocery while my little buddy dropped off smokes at their competitor's across the street.

It was still hot, but the sun had begun to lose some of its bite. And I wasn't as dopey as I had been. The nervous man who wanted me to kill his employee or his boss or his business partner—whichever category Max fit into—seemed a trifle out of focus now. I decided I hadn't played that encounter as well as I might have. At the time I was more strung out than I'd realized.

Dehydration, probably. Maybe I should carry a water jug

on these summer stakeouts. And a bucket of ice to keep the water—or, hey, juice—cool. Better yet, an ice chest in the backseat, with a couple of six-packs—

And then we were on the move again, trundling up Lemmon Avenue toward Love Field.

Two more stops on Lemmon, then Bartelles turned left into a sparse industrial area. We made a series of turns that didn't seem to be taking us anywhere logical. The truck slowed, sped up, then slowed again. I dropped way back now; this was no time to spook him.

Eventually the truck braked sharply and slewed to a sloppy stop, half-on and half-off the wrong side of the road. Bartelles got out, stood by the truck with his hands on his hips, and slowly looked around.

He had picked a good spot. A dozen scrub trees blocked the view from the north and west. The road ran south for fifty yards through open land, then turned east. The only structure with a view of Bartelles and the truck was a long, low, metal building eighty yards back.

That building faced away from Bartelles, and besides, it looked empty, possibly deserted. There were no windows in the back wall, only a stretch of corrugated iron with a single padlocked door. Empty asphalt, a loose jumble of rusty pipes, a stack of rotting pallets, and a big ABCO trash container.

The Mustang and I were hidden behind the trash container.

I had already taken two pictures of Bartelles by then, both of them reasonably tight and clear once the long lens of my dented old Minolta had dragged him up close to me. I snapped him again as he nodded his head twice and turned to stride briskly toward the stand of trees.

When I took the camera away from my eye, I couldn't see him. There was too much contrast between the bright sun and the dark tree shadows. But he was still visible through the Minolta, and I clicked away steadily as he used his pocketknife to saw through his belt and free the chain connected to the large leather wallet that held the company money.

Bartelles put the cash in a plastic bag he took from his pants pocket, then threw away the wallet with an artistic flip of his wrist. Then he took off his shoes, walked gingerly to the far end of the small forest, and buried the bag of cash under loose dirt at the base of a tree.

When he'd walked just as carefully back to where he'd dumped the wallet, he ripped the front of his shirt and threw himself down on the ground. He rolled around in the dirt for a minute, scrunching his back against the ground like a dog. *I fought 'em, boss. Like a tiger, I swear. But they were just too strong for me.*

Bartelles got up, looked around, and found something on the ground, probably a rock. Whatever it was, he dragged it sharply across his forehead three times. He winced noticeably each time.

Finally he stood still for a moment, apparently thinking; then he let his shoulders sag, and he staggered out into the sunlight again.

It was quite a performance, well worth the full roll of thirty-six exposures I'd run through the camera.

By the time I'd followed the road around to the parked truck, Bartelles was standing in the middle of the road. When I stopped, he developed a bad limp and waved his arms feebly.

"Help," he cawed. "I've been robbed."

I leaned over and opened the passenger door. "Get in, Camille."

He threw himself in, babbling about his ordeal, saying

take me to the cops and oh, my Gawd and things like that. During all that he mopped at his gashed forehead with a handkerchief and made sure I noticed his grievous wound.

After five minutes, though, when I hadn't said anything and had driven past two patrol cars, Bartelles pursed his lips and said calmly, "You wanna tell me what the fuck is going on here?"

"You've been a ba-a-a-d boy."

"What are you, pal, a cop or something?"

"Private," I said. "Shanahan will tell you all about it."

"Shanahan! That bastard. Hired you to catch me, huh?"

"Yup." Power repartee à la Gary Cooper.

Bartelles said, "You oughta know, pal, my brother-in-law is very big down at the local. Very big."

"Yup."

"You a union man, pal?"

"Federated Guild of Thugs and Leg-breakers," I said. "I'm on the committee negotiating our new contract."

"Get fucked," he said.

"Good idea for a contract provision. It beats the hell out of overtime and sick pay. You think your brother-in-law could give us a hand with that?"

Our relationship soured after that. He didn't call me pal again, for one thing. And he tried to kick me on the shin when I trotted him into Shanahan's office.

Grinning, Shanahan offered him a quick way out with a hastily typed letter of resignation and confidential confession. Bartelles spit on Shanahan's desk, so we did it the hard way.

It took several hours to recover the cash and the truck and help the cops assemble the small mountain of paperwork they needed to put one petty thief in the slammer. A sergeant named Worthington ramrodded the job; we'd been rookies together years ago. Worthington didn't like my wisecracks about terminal writer's cramp.

It was after nine-thirty that night, and the temperature was down to bearable, when I finally got away from all that heavy-duty crime busting. I had missed the planned candle-light Italian dinner with Hilda, which was bad. I phoned her a few hours back, though, and she'd suggested Whoppers and double onion rings whenever I could make it. Which was good.

Tomorrow, I wouldn't have to chase that stupid truck around town, which was also good. And Shanahan's check lay heavy in my wallet. Another good.

As the Mustang clattered along, I wondered whether the mysterious Max had enjoyed his day. I decided he could not have fully appreciated it, if only because he didn't know how close he had come to running out of days to enjoy.

3

"No kidding, Hil, it was very weird," I said. "I was halfway zonked from the heat and ..."

I grabbed my tray and balanced my hamburger, fries, and beer can while Hilda climbed back into bed. It was a fascinating climb. The water bed sloshed and jiggled, which gave Hilda a strangely awkward grace during the maneuver. Then there was the way the bedside lamp threw highlights on to her skin and—

"Weird certainly seems the word for it," Hilda said. "More wine, please. And why the funny look?"

"Mute admiration. Would you consider crawling in and out of bed like that for the next thirty minutes or so?"

"Absolutely out of the question," Hilda said. I poured more chablis into her glass. She ate an onion ring. I watched her and realized she was the only person I ever watched do an everyday thing like chew.

"You're trying to be cool," I said, "and that's okay. No need to admit you're a pushover for a high-stepper with a sackful of hamburgers."

"You're incredible. Let's get back to the weird part, please. This man actually hired you to kill someone?"

"Yeah. Well, apparently he had already hired the real guy over the phone. He screwed up the meet somehow and thought I was whoever he had talked to." I drank a little beer and struck a pose. "Can't figure out how he could make a mistake like that, though. What with me being such a mild-mannered, unassuming fellow …"

"Don't kid yourself, Ugly," Hilda said. "If appearance was the only criterion, I could book you for two or three ax murders a week."

"I know the antique business is cutthroat, but—"

"But what about the victim, this man Max somebody? Have you told the police yet?"

"First thing in the morning," I said. "There's no screaming hurry. Max is okay until Thursday night at least."

"And you're not going to get involved?" Hilda said. She sounded skeptical.

"What's to get involved with? The cops will go to Max and give him a description of the guy I met today. Max will say oh, damn, that sounds like Barney or Joe or Isran Paderewski and—"

"Isran Paderewski?"

"Whatever. The point is, Max will recognize the nervous guy. Zap! The guy goes straight to slammer city, whereupon he babbles out the name of his would-be hit man, soon-to-be cell-mate. Eventually, six months or a year from now, Ed Durkee will remind me I'm supposed to testify in the Whoosit case the next day."

"And you'll get grumpy because you'll have to wear a tie."

"Yeah, that's the downside of the courtroom number. Damned assistant DAs always want you to wear a tie."

"And that's all you're going to do?" Hilda said. "No poking around just to see what will happen? No helping this Max person because he sounds like a nice guy?"

"Hilda, come on! This is classic cop work. There's nothing here for me. No fee, even."

"Uh-huh." She ate another onion ring.

I took a big bite of my double-beef-and-cheese Whopper; a dollop of sauce squished out and dribbled down my chest. As I stretched to grab a napkin, I dropped the Whopper into my lap.

Hilda laughed.

"I just had this great idea," I said. "I think I'll take a shower."

Hilda laughed again.

I said, "Play your cards right, cookie, and I'll let you join me."

"You never know your luck, big fella."

"Better yet," I said, "let's take a bath instead of a shower. I'll show you how a torpedo works."

She shook her gorgeous head. "You're an animal, Rafferty. An absolute animal."

"I can't help it," I said. "It's a gift."

4

Wednesday morning. I was shaving when Hilda appeared in the mirror. Well, in her bathroom doorway, really. She wore a dark gray business-lady outfit that set off her black hair. She looked great.

"Rafferty," she said, "you'll have to stop at your house before you go into town. You've run out of clean clothes here."

"There's nothing left in the drawer?"

She shook her head. "Only a ripped Dallas Cowboys jersey and those awful cutoff jeans you wore when you cut the grass last week."

"And you thought I was out of clothes."

———

My house on Palm Lane was hot and stuffy, even at nine in the morning. I hadn't been home for twenty-four hours, and the little cottage predated central air-conditioning. But then, so did my landlady.

Mrs. Jorgenson was a widow—a widder woman, old-time Texans would say—and she had firm views about air-conditioning. She didn't believe in contraptions that sucked up all the electricity and spit God-only-knew-what into the air where innocent folks had to breathe it. Still, folks were different now, she knew that, so if I wanted to put in a window unit, it was entirely up to me, but …

I planned to get a window air-conditioner when I could next afford one, but until then I was struggling along by opening all the windows and doors whenever it got hot. That wasn't a bad method, actually. It was unusual for me to be home during the day, the cross-ventilation through the house was good, and there were shade trees all around.

Come to think of it, maybe Mrs. Jorgenson had the right idea.

Anyway, the kitchen door was wide open while I was back in the bedroom changing clothes, so that's probably how the cat got in. I found it crouched in the center of the kitchen floor. It was a good-size cat, one of the orange-and-yellow, faintly striped kind. It froze, belly lowered almost to the floor, and looked at me steadily. It was alert, not afraid. I hadn't realized cats had such large eyes.

"How you doing, cat?" I slowly put down the bag of dirty clothes and squatted in the doorway from the hall to the kitchen. I was eight feet from the cat. It continued to stare at me. Big, big eyes on that thing.

Then the tip of the cat's tail quivered briefly; it whirled and went out the back door. Fast. Okay, "in a blur" is a cliché, but the cat really was that fast.

"Great moves, cat," I said, three seconds behind the action.

Five minutes later, while I shoveled clothes into the machine, there was a flash of orange as the cat came out of a bush in my yard and went over the back fence. That fence was almost six feet high. The cat's jump was the same as me hopping from a sidewalk into a third-story window. Flat-footed. Without apparent effort.

Later yet, on the way to the office, I decided not to dwell on that comparison. Because, never mind the third-story window, I couldn't get over the stupid *fence* and make it look that easy.

———

"Ed, what can I say? I'm reporting a crime. Well, a planned crime anyway. Don't you remember the part about being my friend the policeman?"

"Rafferty," Lieutenant Ed Durkee said slowly, "if this is another of your ..." Pregnant pause, doubtless intended to induce fear and trembling.

I yawned down the phone at him.

"Okay, okay," he said wearily. "Go ahead."

"Your faith in me is touching. Now let's suit up and do a little crime busting." I read Ed the penciled address on the index card the nervous man had given me. "That's half a block off Walnut Hill Lane, Ed. I've already crisscrossed it to a grocery store named, you should excuse the expression, Mini-Maxi Food Barn Number Three. And you'll no doubt be happy to know there are other Mini-Maxi Food Barns conveniently located throughout the metro—"

"The guy wrote this down for you?"

"Yeah. He used block letters, though, so I don't think you're gonna do any good with a handwriting match once you nail him. Oh, and this card spent most of yesterday in two very sweaty pockets: his and mine. You may have a small problem with fingerprints."

"It's never easy with you, is it?" He sighed. Ed does a

great sigh. It goes well with his hound-dog jowls and rumpled brown suits. "Bring me the card, Rafferty. And expect to hang around here for an hour or so. We'll need a full statement."

"I'll be over later. Uh, you did get the timing on this, Ed? Because tomorrow night, when Max doesn't get whacked, this guy's going to wonder why. He might get a little goosey then."

"I've got all that. Bring the card over here."

"On feet of wings, *mon ami*. Anything to bolster the valiant blue line holding back the—" Ed hung up in the middle of *valiant*. He misses some of my best stuff that way.

I hung up, too, and worked on a full report of the Bartelles surveillance. Shanahan wanted all the juicy details for his files. And besides, I told myself, if Bartelles's lawyer had flunked Plea Bargaining 101, this thing might even get to court. Wouldn't I look impressive on the witness stand with a typed report?

I have to give myself silly incentives like that, because I hate writing reports. That may be because I'm not very good at reports. Correction: scratch "not very good," insert "terrible."

Years ago, when I was still on the force, an ulcer-prone bureaucratic patrol lieutenant wrote an evaluation report that said I "failed to show an appreciation for the need to employ sufficiently circumspect language and phraseology in the preparation of official documentation." No kidding, that's what it said.

A week later I slipped an arrest report past him with the help of a records clerk who did the lieutenant's initials better than the lieutenant. That report meandered through the system for three days before someone read it carefully and rocketed it back to the lieutenant with an asbestos memo attached.

As far as I could tell, the lieutenant never worked out why he had okayed my arrest report wherein his beloved phrase "apprehended the alleged perpetrator" had become "nailed that scuzzball cold." He was sucking Mylanta bottles pretty heavily for a while there.

It cost me another poor performance evaluation but it was worth it.

Reminiscences like that slowed down Shanahan's report considerably. By eleven-thirty I couldn't stand to look at all that paper any longer. I stuffed it into my desk drawer to age, grabbed the roll of Bartelles film, and hit the street.

First stop was a fast-photo place where they know me well enough to ask what kind of pictures are going to come out of their fancy machine. I told Ralph this was a G-rated roll. He let his daughter run it through.

Killing time till the prints were ready, I grabbed a sandwich, then browsed through a gun shop across the street. They had a big yellow display bin of those collapsible spring blackjacks that look like fat radio antenna. The bin had a sign that screamed THIRTY PERCENT OFF at me.

When I successfully resisted the sign, the clerk stopped polishing the glass countertop and tried to sell me a fake pocket pager that came apart to reveal a .25 automatic.

I told him, when they brought out a fake ballpoint pen that came apart to reveal a twelve-gauge shotgun, I'd buy one of those. He grunted and went back to work on his countertop. He had a practiced, almost automatic, motion.

"Let me guess," I said. "You used to be a bartender."

"Still am," he said. "Nights."

You can't fool a trained detective like me.

Twenty minutes later I picked up the Bartelles prints and went back to the office, feeling virtuous because I intended to finish that miserable report. That afternoon. Without fail.

Without fail, maybe, but not without pause. Beth Woodland, from the insurance office next door, stopped by with a huge chunk of angel food cake. I was gracious enough to offer both my professional opinion on the cake and a cup of coffee to go with her slice.

Back to Shanahan's report for an hour, then Duane made his monthly visit. Duane's a Korean war vet, so he's getting on now. He came back home on a DC-4, he says, one of the old four-engine propeller airlines. There were no seats on Duane's flight. Only stretchers.

The flight was where they lost his leg, Duane claims. He says they probably sent it to Seattle or somewhere, because that's what they do with suitcases all the time. And how am I doing at finding it? He always asks. Am I getting any closer?

Duane doesn't quite have both oars in the water, of course. When his leg was blown off, the same Chinese artillery round sent a steel sliver whirling into his temple. He lives out in Garland with two unmarried daughters and makes the trip into downtown Dallas every four or five weeks.

When Duane comes to see me, we review The Mysterious Case of the Missing Leg. I tell him I have a hot new lead and, boy, is he gonna get a monster bill when I finally find that leg. Then we talk about soldiering, cars, whatever. After a while Duane gives me a quirky grin and stumps away to catch his bus. The whole process only takes half an hour or so. What the hell, it's probably good for both of us.

What with coffeeklatching with Beth and chasing legs with Duane, it was almost four o'clock by the time Shanahan's report was as good as it was ever gonna get. I borrowed

Beth's photocopier to make my copy—when you type like I do, you don't try fancy stuff like carbons—then I put everything in a manila envelope and mailed it to Shanahan.

Finally I went to the cop shop to see Ed Durkee.

That's when the day started to go down the gurgler.

5

Ed Durkee's office looked the same: DPD blond-bland decor; Ed behind his cluttered desk; Sergeant Ricco sprawled in a chair, dressed for a *Guys and Dolls* fantasy weekend.

The atmosphere in Ed's office made gloom-and-doom sound like a football cheer.

"What the hell is wrong with you two?" I said.

"Give me the index card, Rafferty," Ed said. "Then get out of here." His voice had a bitter edge to it.

"What is this? Are you trying for a personal best in surly?"

Ed shrugged. Ricco said, "Fuck off, Rafferty."

"What about that statement you wanted?"

"Forget it," Ricco said. "Go on, get out of here."

"Not yet." I flipped the nervous man's index card onto Ed's desk, grabbed the empty visitor's chair, and planted myself in it. "I want to prolong these precious moments of unbridled camaraderie."

Ricco sneered. "You know, Ed, the thing about Rafferty that pisses me off the most—I mean *really* pisses me off—is when he does that intellectual-superiority number. Like just then, with big words and a line of high-tone bullshit. It's like he's saying: these dumb cops don't know what I'm talking about, so …" Ricco sighed or grunted; it was hard to tell which. He shifted his chair and stared at Ed's windowsill.

I said, "Ed, do you want to talk about this? Whatever *this* is."

Ed shook his head; his jowls wobbled.

"Ed, *can* you talk about this?"

Ed seemed to think about that. Ricco perked up and watched us, flicking his small eyes from Ed to me and back again. After fifteen seconds Ed shook his head again.

I nodded. "Understood. Where's the heat coming from? Internal, state, feds, what?"

Ed raised one big hand, palm down, and rocked it back and forth in a six-of-one, half-dozen-of-the-other gesture.

"Well, that's too bad, but …" I stood up and looked at Ed and Ricco. Neither of them looked back. "Hell with it," I said, "I'll leave you to your hemlock cups. If you survive, give me a call. I'll spring for a beer or something."

It was pretty obvious what had happened. That morning I had dropped a nice, easy attempted murder case in Ed's lap. Since then someone with clout had taken it away. Office politics. But why were Ed and Ricco taking it so badly? They'd been around long enough—

"I have been ordered to tell you something." Ed's voice stopped me before I cleared the doorway.

I said, "Why do I think I won't like this?"

Ed spoke in a dull monotone, like a bad newscaster with a slow TelePrompTer. "The department appreciates your report and this physical evidence." Ed picked up the index card. The gesture was mechanical and out of phase with his words. "Our investigation is under way. A nonpolice presence would impede that investigation. Accordingly you are instructed not to go to or contact any person at or regarding …" Ed droned the address from the card, then looked up at me. "Is that clear?"

"Why are you so goddamned defensive?" I said. "Look, it's not my case, for god's sake. Do whatever you— Wait a minute! Have you told this guy Max that somebody wants him hit?"

Ed said, "Our investigation is under—"

"Are you *going* to tell him?"

"—way. A nonpolice presence would—"

"One of you better tell me right now that this bullshit is not your idea, Ed."

"—impede that investigation. Of course it's not my idea, Rafferty. For Christ's sake! Now go away, will you?"

"And stay away," Ricco said. "This thing is already so screwed up that you'd only be—"

"Shut up, Ricco," Ed said wearily. "Good-bye, Rafferty."

"I'm going," I said, and I did. After a dozen steps, though, I went back and stuck my head into the office. "Ed, maybe you should cover your ass on this one. Tell the heavy hitters upstairs that I got the message."

Ed turned his big head toward me. "They don't know you like I do," he said. "They'll assume that means you're willing to let it go."

"Serve 'em right, won't it?"

6

wandered out of the downtown cop shop wondering why whoever was pulling Ed's chain didn't want to protect Max, the unlucky potential victim. I found myself thinking of him that way: Max the Unlucky, like Erik the Red or Peter the Great.

On the other hand, Ed's chain puller might know things about Max the Unlucky that I didn't. Maybe I should be comparing him to Vlad the Impaler. Maybe Max was someone the cops wanted, and I had just wandered into the line of fire.

And the timing was still a factor. Max wasn't hurt yet. It would be tomorrow night at least, maybe the morning after, before the nervous man—whoever *he* was—even realized I wasn't the person he'd hired on the phone. After that he would have to find the right man, set up another date and time, then …

Max wouldn't become truly unlucky for another two or three days.

Even so, he should be told. Now.

Then I remembered a biker gang leader named Guts

Holman. If Guts was still alive and I learned that someone wanted to kill him, would I tell Guts?

Never.

So, what if Max the Unlucky was another Guts Holman? Still …

———

For once my timing was impeccable. As I started to pull over to the curb in front of Gardner's Antiques, Hilda's red BMW poked its nose out of the driveway. I waved her out in front of me, then pulled up beside her at the first stoplight.

I draped myself out the Mustang's window, pounded on the door with both hands, and leered at her, panting heavily.

Hilda pretended to ignore me. In a station wagon behind her two women with a carload of kids looked nervous. The woman in the front passenger seat reached up and locked her door.

The light changed. Hilda went straight ahead, gunning it. The station wagon turned onto the cross street, but its turn signal didn't come on until it was halfway around the corner.

I caught Hilda at the next light and pulled up alongside. Her passenger window hummed down. She said, "Don't you do that again."

"Wouldn't think of it. Perhaps you'd like to hear my famous timber wolf howl, however."

"No way."

"I could do it pianissimo. To keep from embarrassing you."

"You're too late," Hilda said.

"Oh. Well, then, you wanna go drink and eat, babe?"

"For a Neanderthal, you're a smooth talker. Lead on, big guy."

After wriggling through a few of my favorite shortcuts, we merged our way onto Stemmons Freeway. It was busy—the rush hour loads Stemmons up pretty badly sometimes. We eventually came to the exit I wanted and took it. Hilda followed me into the cluster of restaurants a block off Walnut Hill Lane.

I waved her up alongside me. "Pick a beanery, any beanery."

Hilda shrugged. "Mother Tucker's?"

Four minutes later a clean-cut young waiter gave me a beer to play with while he opened a bottle of chardonnay for Hilda. He went through the full routine, label-checking and cork-pulling and sample-pouring and ice-bucketing. I think he stretched the wine business out some, so he could be around Hilda longer. I could not fault his judgment.

Hilda had had a good afternoon. She scooped up a bargain at an estate auction. "You should see it," she said. "A large French Empire mantel clock. Perfect condition. You'd hate it."

"What is it, one of those ornate things with gimcracks and swirls and doohickeys everywhere?"

"Pretty much. I don't care for the style, either, but I have a hungry buyer waiting for it." She sipped her wine and smiled to herself.

It was too early to eat yet. Next time the waiter came to top up Hilda's wineglass, we ordered a plate of snack food and wondered aloud how a dentist in Odessa, Texas, became a freak for Napoleonic timepieces. We decided it didn't matter how, as long as he bought them from Hilda. The snacks came. I sent the waiter after another beer for me, and I poured Hilda's wine this time. The waiter looked jealous.

Hilda popped a toasted cheese something into her mouth and chewed happily. "So, beloved savage," she said, "how was your day?"

I told her. She wasn't very happy with Ed and Ricco.

"That's just not right," she said. "They should do something."

"What would you suggest?"

"They should tell this man Max." She didn't seem to have any doubts about that.

The waiter brought my new beer. I drank some. "Police departments tend to get angry when cops disobey direct orders, Hil."

"What could happen to them?" she said. "What's the worst thing?"

"Getting kicked off the force is always the worst thing for career cops. That probably wouldn't happen, though. Suspension, maybe."

"*Probably?* You mean there's even a small chance a police officer could get fired for not letting someone get killed?" Hilda snorted. "That's insane!"

"No, it isn't. At least, it might not be. And you asked what was the worst thing."

She bristled up to argue. I shushed her. I wanted to try my Guts Holman argument on her, but without mentioning Guts. Hilda doesn't like to be reminded of those bikers.

"Try this for a what-if," I said. "What if Max is mob connected? And what if the state or federal fuzz is about to nail Max and his pals? And finally what if a cop popped up and told Max to watch his back 'cause somebody out there doesn't like him? Blooey! Months, maybe years, of police work go down the drain. Don't you think somebody should have a long, hard talk with that cop?"

"That's ridiculous," Hilda said. "The mob wouldn't try to hire you to kill this Max person. They'd do it themselves. And why would they want to, if he was one of them?"

"Come on, Hil. I only made up one possibility. I don't know what's actually happening."

Messed up again, Rafferty. You should have gone with the Guts Holman argument in the beginning.

Hilda crunched a celery stalk like she was mad at it. "Your cop friends are boxed in. That's what you're saying, isn't it?"

"Yeah. And it bugs the hell out of them," I said.

"But you're not boxed in, because the police department can't fire you. Not again anyway."

"True. One to a customer, and they took their best shot years ago."

Hilda said, "That's why we came all the way out here to eat. Because the Micro-Multi whatever—"

"Mini-Maxi Food Barn Number Three," I said. "Please. Somebody worked hard to think up a name like that."

"The Mini-Maxi Food Barn, then, is—"

"Number Three."

She ignored me. "—is around here somewhere close."

"Well …"

"And after dinner tonight, you're going to warn this Max, whoever he is. Because someone might kill him tomorrow night."

"As it happens, I do need a loaf of bread. While I'm buying bread, I might say hello to Max. If I should happen to see him."

Hilda nodded shortly. "For once I think you're doing the right thing."

"You modern women are such a disappointment. Used to be, women said great stuff, like 'My hero!' Now what do I get? 'I think you're doing the right thing.'" I took a long swig of beer and shook my head. "The hero business just ain't what it used to be."

Hilda clasped her hands over her heart, fluttered her eyelids, and trilled fervently, "Sir Rafferty; my hero!"

"That's better," I said. "Now where's that goddamned dragon?"

7

The Mini-Maxi Food Barn was classier than I had expected. Out front, between the parking lot and the street, there was a large sign shaped like a traditional barn. The sign was red with white lettering, lighted from inside and mounted on a hefty pylon. The sign revolved slowly and dragged large splotches of bright light across the parking lot. You wouldn't want to live across the street from that sign.

The store building was set back behind fifty feet of asphalt parking lot. Maybe sixty feet. Enough for almost twenty parking slots, anyway, which seemed like overkill for a late-night convenience store, but what did I know about the food business?

The Mini-Maxi Food Barn really was a barn, provided you could accept a too-low, too-narrow barn sitting sideways on the lot, with plate glass windows and sliding doors on the street side. One end wasn't square with the long sides. That end was slewed toward the street; angled so passersby could admire the big barn doors and the hayloft port and the pole above the port to lift up the hay. The Mini-Maxi Food Barn was bucolic as hell in its own special way. The Waltons meet Madison Avenue.

Need I mention that the building was painted red?

Considering there were apparently three of these things, the operation looked professional. Twee, but professionally so.

It didn't seem to do much business, though. I hadn't seen any customers yet. To be fair, though, my in-depth commercial and financial survey was based on only two trips around the block.

I was going around in circles like that because I wanted to find the dedicated cops who were so intensely involved with the place that I had been warned off. It didn't matter, I guess. Not really. If they were there, I'd still go in, but I'd be sneakier about it.

Past the Mini-Maxi again. The parking lot was still empty. This time I noticed the big sign said the store hours were six a.m. to midnight seven days a week. That was probably a dig at 7-Eleven. Ah, the cutthroat world of commerce.

I made the third circuit a bigger square; two blocks on a side this time. Still didn't see any vans with portholes, doorway loungers, or men sitting quietly in parked cars.

Which did not necessarily mean there was no surveillance of the Mini-Maxi. I couldn't check everywhere. Take the store and shops across the street, for example. Half of them were two-story buildings; a long-lens camera could be hidden behind any of those windows.

And that was only the looking. Listening would be even easier. I bet myself I could put three bugs within six feet of the cash register and pay for a quart of ice cream at the same time. With the correct change.

Come on, Rafferty, stop daydreaming and go to work.

I didn't make a full circuit that time. I stopped short and

parked around the corner from the store. That Mini-Maxi parking lot was too bright. Any halfway decent camera team would have my license plate number in a fiftieth of a second, my name in five minutes, and Ed Durkee on the carpet first thing in the morning.

So I walked to the store, thinking they might give Ed and me a hard time yet, but at least they'd have to work for it. Screw 'em.

I found myself thinking "screw 'em" more and more often about more and more things. Hilda said that was part of an accelerated aging process; I was becoming a curmudgeon before my time. I said my continued life experience gave me new insights into reality. Hilda was probably right. Screw 'em anyway.

As I crossed the bright parking lot, I kept my face turned toward the Mini-Maxi. The camera jockeys could take all the pictures of the back of my head they wanted.

A bell bonged softly as I stepped through the open entrance doors. The class act continued inside; the vinyl tile floor was spotless, the display gondolas were well spaced, and the food on them was neatly arranged. Half the back wall was taken up with glass-fronted cold storage; dairy products, dips, soft drinks, juice. There was a low magazine stand, a neighborhood bulletin board, a bread rack; all the usual convenience store items.

I snagged a loaf of whole wheat off the bread rack and headed for the cash register counter at the right-hand end of the building. I hadn't seen anyone yet. Maybe Max was back in the storeroom. I harrumphed twice. Nothing.

What was I supposed to do? Holler, "Hey, Max, wait till you hear this. A guy wants to ..."

I harrumphed again instead.

Then it occurred to me that this might be Max's night off.

After all, he wasn't scheduled to get whacked until tomorrow. Which led me to the next cheerful thought. If Max wasn't here, who was? The nervous man who wanted Max hit? Naw, that wouldn't be a problem. I could con my way out of—

Then I glanced down the last aisle, between a gondola loaded with chips and crackers and the cold storage unit. The man I saw there was Max, I guessed. Had to be Max.

For a long, sick second, I thought I'd mistaken the date; that this was Thursday night, not Wednesday. But I wasn't a day late; this was still Wednesday.

Not that it mattered much to the man who had to be Max.

He couldn't get any deader tomorrow night.

8

was furious, which was a strange emotion for me when standing over the corpse of a total stranger. I could remember other feelings associated with bodies I'd discovered, or seen later, or created on the spot, but I couldn't recall this pure blind anger.

I was angry at myself, probably, but I can rationalize as well as anyone else. So I thought I was angry at the cops.

I yelled, "Get in here, you dumb bastards! Come see what you caused."

Nothing happened. The empty store had a hollow back ground hum that was alternately annoying and soothing. The only other sound was a hoarse, rasping noise. I finally realized that was me, breathing.

Think, Rafferty. If this place was bugged, the cops would have heard Max get it. They'd already be here. You dummy.

Cameras, then. I stalked out the front door and waved broadly at the building across the street. *Come here. This way. Follow me.* No matter how they interpreted it, that much arm-flailing should bring even the sleepiest rookie trotting this way any second.

Nobody came.

Well, goddamn.

There really weren't any cops out there. None. Not hiding and watching, not taking pictures, not listening. None at all.

How 'bout them apples?

Most of the household goods were down at the end of the central gondola. I opened a pack of rubber kitchen gloves first, put them on—they were yellow, very chic—then I found a note pad and a felt-tip pen and cellophane tape and a garbage bag.

I wrote, "SORRY, CLOSED FOR CLEANING," on a sheet of paper and taped it inside the window. Then I closed the door and looked for the key.

It seemed like a long time before I found three keys on a ring in a junk drawer behind the cash register counter. The keys had been tossed in on top of paper scraps, a receipt book, scissors, string, and—well, well, well—a Model 65 Smith & Wesson .38 revolver.

The gun could wait. I locked the doors. Good. Now I had breathing room.

Back at the junk drawer I decided the gun probably didn't mean anything. Convenience stores are an armed robbers natural grazing ground. There were probably guns under most cash register counters. Hell, if I worked in a place like this, I'd have a machine gun. And grenades.

I sniffed the muzzle of the Smith anyway; it had not been fired since it was last cleaned. And it had not been cleaned for a very long time.

I went to see the sad little man sprawled prone on the tile floor. He lay in the curiously flat posture corpses invariably adopt. That must have something to do with the total absence of muscle tension.

The first thing to find out was whether or not this was really Max.

His driver's license said he was Max Krandorff. He was, um, let's see, fifty-seven years old last December, and he lived in Plano, on a street I didn't recognize.

There was money in his wallet. And credit cards. Last thing I'd heard, the hitter was supposed to fake a robbery. Maybe it's true; maybe you can't get good help anymore.

Then it occurred to me that the cash register was closed. I went to it and pushed buttons, trying to get it open. I felt foolish doing that with gaudy yellow kitchen gloves on. If a customer looked in ... but this store didn't seem to have any customers, and that didn't make much sense, either.

I kept stabbing my yellow fingers at the cash register buttons. How could it be so difficult to get one of these gadgets open? It looked so simple when sixteen-year-old clerks did it.

Finally the register *binged* and stuck out its cash drawer tongue at me. There was money in the drawer. Not much money, but I seemed to recall that convenience stores transferred cash from the register to a floor safe three or four times a day. I shut the cash drawer.

The safe was gawd-awful obvious, once I looked for it. It was a barrel safe, concreted into the foundation slab by the front window, with an overhead spotlight shining down on it. The safe was shut.

So what had happened to the fake robbery? Had the hitter been interrupted? I went to see if Max could tell me.

As I started to examine the body closely, the front door rattled. Uh-oh.

A muffled voice yelled, "Hey, open up." The door rattled again as he shook it. "Closed, my ass. You're supposed ..."

I waited there, hiding behind the potato chips, squatting

beside the body. Max and Rafferty, old buddies, him dead and me in my pretty gloves.

Outside, the frustrated customer yelled, "F'chrissake," and kicked the door.

A muscle in the back of my neck quivered and jumped, My scalp felt tight. I said, "He'll give up in a minute," to the body before I realized what I was doing.

Waiting like that was not a whole lot of fun.

The grumbling customer stayed around for two or three minutes, then gave the door a final kick and his curses faded slowly.

I waited a full five minutes, then circled around the end of the gondolas and peeked out into the parking lot. There was no one in sight.

Back to Max yet again.

There was a certain amount of gore. There almost always is. Once you learn to get past the mess, you can usually work out what happened.

The hitter made Max kneel down, then shot him high in the back of the neck. Bye-bye, brain stem. Max pitched forward into the remains of his throat and chin; he was probably dead before he landed. His legs might have straightened as he died, or maybe the killer grabbed Max's ankles and pulled his legs out straight afterward.

Either way Max had also been kneecapped, shot through both knees from behind. I grabbed a handful of trouser cloth and hoisted up his leg. The vinyl floor underneath was scarred but not particularly messy.

Max had fallen with his arms loose; his hands were palm up beside his hips. The killer had chopped the right hand with an ax, a meat cleaver, something like that. Three whole fingers and half of another lay like wrinkled sausages, separated from Max's hand by an inch of gashed tile. Not much blood, though.

Summation: Max was already dead when the hitter kneecapped him and chopped off his fingers. You don't need a pathology degree to recognize wounds inflicted after the heart has stopped pumping. Corpse mutilation, then, not the results of a struggle.

And because the money was still there, the fake-robbery gambit had been dropped. Instead, the hitter or the nervous man, or both, wanted to sell this as a thrill killing. *Booga-booga*, a psycho stalks the night.

Bad move, guys. A grocery store robbery that escalated into murder was brutal but predictable. As a crime, it slotted nicely into a category any cop could accept.

Wandering psychos don't fit, though, and this wasn't even a particularly good wandering-psycho scenario. I could picture Ricco in here later tonight. He would look around and think and finally sneer. He would probably say it didn't "make no god-damned sense."

And Ricco would be right. This didn't make no goddamned sense. So I tried to find something that did.

There was a desk and a bulletin board in one corner of the back room. Half the company memos on the board had been signed by Max Krandorff. Someone named Carl Dresden had signed the others. There were also dog-eared price lists and work rosters—Max was clerking two nights a week, which seemed odd for a guy who made company policy—and there were lists of phone numbers and business cards for various repair firms and wholesalers. One of the cards belonged to a sales rep from Shanahan's tobacco and candy company. Talk about your small world.

Mostly the things in the desk were junk—matches, half-empty cigarette packs, an old *Penthouse*, things like that. But the grand prize was in the desk, too, tucked away in the bottom drawer.

It was a glossy brochure called "The Mini-Maxi Story: a guide for employees." The cover had a color photograph of two men standing in front of a Food Barn. They had their arms thrown over each other's shoulders and they grinned self-consciously at the camera.

One of the men was Max Krandorff. The other was the nervous man who wanted Max dead. The picture caption said: "Mr. Krandorff and Mr. Dresden at the grand opening of the second Mini-Maxi Food Barn."

Carl Dresden, read my lips: Gotcha!

I folded the brochure lengthwise and shoved it into my hip pocket. That was the last interesting item I found. When I ran out of places to look, I unlocked the front doors, put the keys back in the junk drawer, and removed the CLOSED sign. I put the sign, the note pad, the tape, the gloves, all the things I'd used, into the garbage bag.

I ducked out the back door, walked around the corner, and unlocked the Mustang. The garbage bag went into the trunk and I hid the brochure under the seat. The Mustang started first try; new points and plugs last week. I drove back toward the Mini-Maxi store.

Eleven o'clock on a warm clear evening. Peaceful. Half a long block away, traffic flickered by on Walnut Hill Lane, but there were no cars here. I pulled into the parking lot, stopped near the door, and went inside.

Imagine my shock and surprise when I found a dead body in there. Truly. A *dead body.*

Naturally I looked for a phone to call the police right away.

9

checked each aisle and the back room to make sure no one had wandered in. The Mini-Maxi was too quiet to expect anything unusual like a customer, but a tourist might have dropped by. A couple from Michigan: perhaps, wanting directions to J. R.'s ranch.

But there was only Max, still sprawled beside the Fritos like an exhibit in a punk-art gallery. *Max, sans throat, kneecaps and fingers:* a confrontational work.

It seemed to be taking minimalism a little too far.

I was getting punchy. Wednesday was becoming another long day. I grabbed the phone to tell the cops about Max. Whoops, not Max, that poor man in aisle three. Gotta remember I'm not supposed to know who he is.

In the same spirit, I didn't worry about fingerprints now; I was here legitimately.

Verisimilitude, thy name is Rafferty.

But when the police emergency number answered, I had second thoughts and hung up. Was I trying to play it too cute? The first uniformed squad might believe I had found Max by accident, but whoever was muzzling Ed Durkee would know better. Tomorrow the heavies would be at the front door before my cornflakes had a chance to sog.

Then, too, I realized for the first time that I had another option. I could walk away. When I had come here to warn Max, I'd expected to run a gauntlet of watching cops. They weren't here. If I wanted, I could not be here, too.

That idea was briefly attractive, but it didn't feel right. Too easy for a tough hombre like me.

I tapped out Ed Durkee's home number. The phone rang six times before he answered it with a grunt.

I said, "Hi, Ed. Asleep, huh?"

"No, Rafferty, it's a game I play. I put on my pajamas, turn out all the lights, and guess who's going to phone me. What the hell do you want?" He yawned loudly.

"Stay awake; this will be worth it. What do you know about the surveillance on the Mini-Maxi place I told you about?"

"Nothing, except it should be tight. They've got enough manpower to stake out all of Oklahoma." Ed's voice was muffled on "Oklahoma." I could imagine him dry-washing his malleable face. "Why?" he said. "You can't figure out how to get in there without being spotted?"

"*Get* in? Ed, I'm already in."

"The hell you say." Ed seemed to wake up in a hurry then.

"The guy got wasted a day early, Ed. The Dudley Do-rights who wouldn't warn him didn't bother to keep an eye on him, either."

Ed sighed. "Jesus, I ... You call the emergency number yet?"

"I kind of figured doing it this way might give you some leverage and save me some hassle. Right or wrong?"

"Right. Give me the number there, and for Christ's sake, Rafferty, don't touch anything. I'll call you back. Five minutes."

Eight minutes later the phone rang. I picked it up but didn't say anything. I had begun to reconsider whether or not I wanted to be here officially. After a few seconds of silence, Ed said, "Rafferty?"

"Yo."

"Are there any civilians there?"

"Only the dead one."

"Does anyone but you know about this?"

"I don't see how they could, Ed. This is the dullest convenience store in captivity."

"Good. Here's the story, then. Those jerk-offs upstairs screwed up, I don't have to tell you that. Personally I think they're about to compound that screwup, but I'm only the messenger tonight."

"And loving it," I said.

"Waiting my turn," he said. "Waiting my turn. Now listen. What I'm going to say is official. From high up, you got that?"

"Hang on a minute," I said. "I'll take one of my heart pills."

"Walk away from it, Rafferty. A team will be there soon—"

"A team? What is this 'team' crap? What happened to a patrol squad, a meat wagon, and whoever's awake down at Homicide? Ed, what is all this?"

I was beginning to think I'd messed up; maybe I should have taken the cut-and-run option.

"You're clean," Ed said. "But they have a four-part message for you. One: Leave the scene immediately."

"That part I like."

"Two: Thank you for cooperating."

"Betcha five dollars they choked on that one."

"No bet. Three: They will contact you in due course. I don't know what 'in due course' means," Ed said.

"On current performance, I'd guess that means late next year."

"Yeah, probably so. And four: Once you've gone away, stay away. Do not do anything or say anything that even remotely involves this case."

"Ed, why are they so uptight?"

He sighed. "You'd have to see it to believe it. Just do what they want, okay? For what it's worth, that would help me out. A lot."

"Okay, but … let me get the last part straight. What if I'm walking down the street tomorrow, and I see the guy who thought I was a hit man? Do I grab him? Or tail him? Or what?"

"You pretend he doesn't even exist. That's the way they want it."

"This is crazy, Ed."

"No shit. Do it, will you? Now get out of there."

"Getting out of here, boss," I said and hung up.

I started out, then went back and wiped the phone clean.

Rafferty's Rule Forty-three: When in doubt, be sneaky. I didn't trust the squirrels running this operation.

I got into the Mustang, fired up, and backed out of the parking lot as a car came down the street. It pulled into the parking lot and took the space beside the one I'd just left. There was one man in the car.

I stopped the Mustang and got out. Despite the "get lost" orders Ed had relayed, I decided to chase away the customer before he found Max's body, then gave the cops my license number or description.

The car was a dark blue Buick four-door. The driver got out carrying an attaché case. He bounced the handle in his fingers as he walked toward me.

It was Carl Dresden, Max's murderous partner, and he had a wide smile on his face.

10

Carl Dresden said, "It's done, then? You're, uh, finished?" He stood well away from me, a full step farther than normal. Couldn't blame him, though. Most people would stand back from someone they thought was a hit man fresh from the kill.

Dresden's round face suddenly sagged; he looked apprehensive. "You have done it, haven't you? He's not still, um, alive in there?"

"No," I said.

This was not going to be easy. I wanted to feed this jerk a knuckle sandwich, then cart him off to the slammer. Ed Durkee wanted me to do what his superiors ordered: pretend Dresden wasn't there.

Still, how wrong could it be to say one little word?

So I said, "No," again. And I added, "He's not alive." Sometimes I take liberties.

Dresden let out his breath in a long, loud sigh. "Good." He nodded his head rapidly a dozen times or more. He nodded without emotion or meaning, like those nodding plastic dogs you see in car windows. "I hate it that this had to happen,"

Dresden said, "but when a partner does what Max did ... well, like I said last night, what can you do?"

That sounded intriguing. *You said that last night, did you, Carl? And to whom did you say that, pray tell?* But I played it the way Ed wanted. I only clucked my tongue and echoed Dresden. "What can you do?"

"Darn right," he said. He'd lost the flop-sweat nervousness of our downtown meeting. He seemed bright tonight, even chipper. Apparently having your partner killed did wonders for the old motivation.

Dresden said, "I hope I didn't mess up on the phone, You weren't alone, huh? I mean, that's why you pretended we hadn't met, right?"

There was another comment that screamed out for elaboration. *Arrgh!*

Dresden took a cautious step closer and held out the attaché case. "Anyway, here," he said.

I took the case. It was getting more and more difficult to pretend he wasn't there. "Thanks," I said. *Oh, Rafferty, you ad-libbing fool you.*

Dresden shrugged "Excuse me," he said, "but I better run now. I'm supposed to be out of town." He grimaced apologetically, nodded several more times, turned, and hurried to the Buick.

I let him go, but it hurt. I felt slow and foolish, like a smart-mouth disk jockey bogged down by a lip full of Novocain.

I memorized Dresden's license number as he started the Buick and pulled out. If Ed and the hotshots "upstairs" didn't like it, that was their problem. When Dresden had gone, I put the case on the hood of the Mustang and clicked open the latches. The case was full of money. Well, not crammed tight, perhaps, but pretty damned full.

I looked at all that cash for a moment, then realized it was way past time for me to be gone. I tossed the case into the backseat of the Mustang and drove away, wondering exactly how much money that was. Had to be ten thousand, maybe twelve.

Not killing Max Krandorff had turned out to be a lucrative job. I should not do it more often.

As I stopped for the light at Walnut Hill Lane, a tan Pontiac hurried around the corner, then slowed to a crawl. There were several men in the Pontiac—four at least, maybe five. One of them shined a powerful flashlight out a window. Checking for street numbers, probably, so he could find the Mini-Maxi Food Barn.

A hundred yards away the giant Mini-Maxi sign swung around and around like a landlocked lighthouse.

Never fear, the team is here.

I drove home and put the money case on my dining room table. Then I got a beer and drank some while I phoned Hilda.

"I was beginning to worry," she said.

"Yeah, well, it got a little more complicated than I expected, babe."

"But you're all right?"

"Sure. No problem."

"What about your relationship with the police?"

"Uh, patchy is perhaps the best word," I said. "It's a long story. Dinner tomorrow, okay? A full and factual account, delivered with my usual witty asides and insightful anecdotes."

"Rafferty, *le raconteur*," Hilda said.

"*Avec fromage,*" I said.

"You nut. Good night."

"Night, Hil."

I drank another beer while I looked at the money case

again. The bills had been separated by denomination and rubber-banded into untidy stacks. Twenties, mostly, though there were several stacks of fifties, too. One stack of tens, three stacks of hundreds. Each stack had a scrap of paper tucked under the rubber band with an amount scrawled on it.

I found the little calculator the gas station gave me last year and added up all the numbers on the paper slips. Fourteen thousand and eight hundred dollars. I must have made a mistake. Fifteen thousand, probably. It was way over the going rate for a simple hit either way.

I put the case in my closet, drank one more beer, and went to bed. I woke up briefly around four-thirty, when the cat yowled and spat outside the window.

Watch your back, cat. It's a goddamned jungle out there.

The cat yowled again. Maybe it already knew that.

11

E d Durkee came to the house at nine-thirty the next morning. He planted his bulk in a chair at the dining room table and accepted a cup of coffee. It was a warm day; almost eighty degrees already. Even so, Ed wore one of his rumpled brown suits.

"You're alone?" I said. "I thought you and Ricco were Siamese twins. Joined at the badge since birth."

"Har, har," he grumped. He sipped his coffee and frowned at the cup. "You're off-limits," he said. "Just talking to you violates a direct order. Ricco doesn't quite have the clout to get around that yet."

"Spare me the turgid tales of department politics, Ed. Been there; done that; bought the T-shirt."

I looked past his shoulder and out into the backyard. The cat had not come back since I'd accidentally spooked it over an hour ago.

"Good point," Ed said. "It's my problem. Fill me in on last night."

"Wait a minute," I said. I got the attaché case and put it on the table. I put the Mini-Maxi employee's guide on top of the case. Max Krandorff and Carl Dresden smiled their glossy aw-shucks smiles up at us.

I tapped Max. "This is the guy who got whacked last night." I tapped Carl. "This is the guy who wanted me to do the whacking. Have you been out there, Ed?"

He grimaced. "No. And don't give me any crap about how you didn't have time to notice any details." He waggled his fingers at me. "Speak to me."

I described the body and told him how the killing and mutilation must have happened.

Ed looked puzzled. "Why the extra touches?"

"Beats me. I thought it was very inconsiderate of him not to leave a note explaining that."

"Uh-huh." Ed prodded the attaché case. "And what's this?"

"An immodest emolument. Fifteen big ones, which is enough too much to tell me Dresden doesn't know zip about hiring a hit man."

"Oh, shit," Ed said. "He showed up last night? At the store?"

"Yeah, I thought that indicated a certain lack of sophistication myself."

"And you didn't try to stop him?"

"I seem to recall very rigid instructions about that," I said.

Ed nodded thoughtfully. "Right. Well, I'll be damned."

"I figured, what the hell, we know who he is. And I got his license number. He won't be hard to find."

"Um," Ed mumbled. He tugged at his lower lip and frowned into space.

"He was naked," I said, "and painted blue, with a pointy clown hat, two electric trains, and a frozen chicken."

"Uh-huh." Ed pulled his lip another half inch out of shape.

I left him to his thoughts. Outside there was still no sign of the cat. I got my breakfast plate out of the sink and carried it into the backyard. I left the plate on the grass, then sat on the back step. Egg yolk and bacon grease should pull the cat out of hiding. Outdoor lore from Bring 'Em Back Alive Rafferty.

After ten catless minutes I heard Ed lumber into the kitchen. I went inside.

"Sorry about that," Ed said. "I'm a little preoccupied about this, uh, situation."

"Do, uh, tell."

He leaned against the. kitchen counter and looked at me. "It's kind of embarrassing," he said.

"I'm tough. It won't bother me."

Ed said, "Me, damn it. I'm the one it embarrasses."

"Yeah, that's what I meant. You want to talk about it or not?"

Ed shook his big head. "Later, maybe." He shuffled his feet. The process vaguely resembled two aircraft carriers changing places at the dock. "Rafferty, how do you feel about me taking that cash? I can't give you a department receipt for it."

"Oh, damn. There goes my condo in Vail."

"Thanks," Ed said. "Well, look, make notes about last night while it's still fresh in your mind. It may take a while, but the grand jury will hear this one. Guaranteed." He sounded like he was trying to convince himself, not me.

"You got it."

Ed pushed himself away from the counter and walked out of the kitchen. As he went through the doorway, he said, "I owe you."

"Write that down," I said. "Sign it."

Twenty minutes later, the cat came out of a bush and

licked the plate. When it had finished, it looked at me for a while, then jumped the fence.

I walked into the yard and picked up the plate. It was spotless

How about that? With a hardworking cat around the place you don't need a dishwasher.

12

I went to the office Thursday afternoon. Mostly I sat around, although I did put in a fast fifteen minutes work on the Smith case. Hah! Some case.

Five months back, I'd been hired by a lawyer to find a nineteen-year-old who had inherited three thousand dollars from an uncle he may or may not have remembered. The kid —his name was John Smith, I swear—didn't know about the money yet. A year ago he had headed out of town with a bicycle, a backpack, and a plan to travel around the world. He failed to specify a starting direction.

Washington admitted Smith had a passport but said there was no record that he'd left the country. That didn't necessarily mean he was still here, though. He could have walked across into Mexico with the tourists. (Or into Canada, which I kept forgetting; down here *border* means Mexico.) Or Smith might have signed onto a tramp freighter or fishing boat; some of them are weak in the record-keeping department.

Mom and Dad Smith didn't know where John was, and they didn't seem to care much. I guess Unk didn't remember them in the will. The parents steered me to an old girlfriend who now lived in Midland, though. Girlfriend was certain she would hear from John sooner or later, because they "were, like, really, really close, you know?"

And there was an aunt in Minnesota with a voice like soft chimes. I always felt good when I talked to her.

I phoned both women every few weeks, but so far neither of them had heard from John Smith. Every other month I billed the lawyer for the long-distance charges and one hour's work. So far he still paid the bills. That wouldn't last.

I put another quarter-hour's labor on the lawyer's tab, then wondered what else I could do to pass the time until tonight's dinner with Hilda.

About then Ricco phoned. "Ed with you?" he said.

"No."

"All right," Ricco said. "I'll find him." There were traffic sounds behind his voice.

"You move your desk out onto the sidewalk for the fresh air?"

"Cute, Rafferty. I just don't trust those ... forget it. If you see Ed, tell him I called."

"Sure. Have you picked up Dresden yet?"

"Don't I wish," Ricco said. "Naw, he's still out there, as far as I know. He ain't at home, anyway."

"Try his office, wherever that is."

"Yeah, that's next," Ricco said.

"I gave Ed a plate number this morning."

"I know. It's a rental. The company's checking now to see where it is." He paused and let me listen to buses for a moment. "Tell you what, Rafferty, I got a bad feeling about this one."

"Be of stout heart, valiant crime fighter."

Ricco blew a raspberry and hung up.

I put my feet on the desk and read for a while. I'd become

addicted to C. S. Forester's Horatio Hornblower novels about that time, so I settled in with good old Horny. Between the two of us, we sank a couple of French frigates in no time at all.

Hornblower and I were pacing the quarterdeck, looking up at the t'gallants, whatever they were, when the phone rang.

"You Rafferty?" a man said aggressively.

"Me Rafferty," I said. "You Jane?"

"What? Uh, maybe I got the wrong number here. Where is this anyway?" His voice ricocheted back and forth between bluster and cunning.

"Just think of me as Superman for the over-twelves. What can I do for you?"

"Over-whats? Superman? What kinda—"

"Scratch Superman," I said. "What do you want?"

"Well, I'm not ... I ..." His voice was suddenly defensive.

I waited; he spluttered and hedged long enough to convince me he didn't know what he wanted. I said, "Let me ask you a question."

"What?" he said. Very wary there. Touchy, touchy.

"What's a t'gallant?"

"Huh?"

"Oh, damn," I said. "And I was so sure you'd know."

He hung up. So did I. Horny and I sank another frigate.

————

That night Hilda and I had one of our dual dinners. She calls them "movable feasts"; I prefer "schizophrenia with gusto."

We did Hilda's half first, at an uptown place where all the wine was imported and there wasn't a word of English on the menu. The place was so classy, I even wore a tie. For Hilda.

I think Liz Browning forgot to write down "wearing a tie" when she counted the ways.

Our waiter was named Philippe—uh-huh—and he thoroughly approved of Hilda's wine selection. He brought me a beer, but pretended he hadn't.

I had been telling Hilda about the Mini-Maxi fiasco. "I suppose you feel responsible for the man being killed," she said.

Philippe showed up with our appetizers then. Mine turned out to be a single deep-fried shrimp in the middle of a big white plate. I ate the shrimp but left the single strand of green pepper and puddle of two-tone sauce. Wouldn't want to get a reputation for being piggy.

I said, "Yeah, I do feel kinda bad about Max."

"Don't." Hilda's appetizer was a thin slice of avocado with a tablespoon of oily vinegar and one strawberry. She took very small bites and made it last a full minute.

I told her how Dresden had appeared out of left field to pay me for killing Max. "And the cops didn't want me to touch him. Strictly hands off. Figure that one out."

Philippe whisked away the appetizer plates and brought our entrees. I almost called him back, but then I found my veal cowering under a slice of tomato. I ate the veal and the tomato.

Hilda tasted her small square of fish. "Um, delicious," she said.

"So was mine."

Philippe brought a small serving plate of vegetables. Hilda took a potato the size of a golf ball. I passed; they didn't look big enough to leave the nest.

Hilda said, "Why can't they catch this man, uh, Dresden. Surely that can't be so difficult."

"No argument there, babe."

"After all, you gave them his name. And a license plate."

"Ricco says he's not home and the car was a rental. And Dresden said something about being out of town. That's his alibi."

"How can that be an alibi if he's not out of town?"

"I'd say he made a big deal out of catching a plane, then came back. He could have driven back or flown back under a different name, depending on how far away he went in the first place. When they find out where the car was rented, they'll know which."

"It seems to me that only tells them which city to search," Hilda said.

I shrugged. "Hell, his office probably knows where he is. And if they don't, it's nothing a few thousand phone calls to hotels won't fix. Police departments are good at that stuff." I finished my beer; Philippe was nowhere in sight. "But they don't really have to do any of that, Hil. Any day now Dresden will rocket back into town, brimming over with crocodile tears about his poor partner, Max."

"So they only need the rental car details to prove later what he did. For the trial."

"You're good, tootsie. Wanna go partners? Rafferty and Gardner: Private Heat. It has a nice ring to it."

"Gardner and Rafferty," she said. "Discreet Investigations for the Truly Discriminating."

"Forget it."

We had dessert; a postage stamp of chocolaty gunk for Hilda; a spoonful of ice cream for me. Philippe brought a big bill in a bigger leather folder. He came back three minutes later and seemed shocked to find I'd put nasty old money in there instead of a pristine credit card. He took the folder away to sterilize it.

Hilda finished her wine. "Anytime," she said.

"Hot damn," I said, "now we can go eat."

———

"That fancy French stuff is okay," I said, "but when you're hungry, it's hard to beat traditional Italian food." I took another bite.

Hilda said, "Pizza and beer hardly traditional Italian cuisine."

"Close enough."

She took another slice of pizza, but not before she'd swiped extra pepperoni from the adjacent slice. "I don't understand all this trouble your friend Ed is having," she said. "Do police really swipe cases from each other?"

"Not normally," I said. "Oh, well, there's always some office politics, of course; any big organization has that. But this is different. Damned if I can figure it out."

"By the way, how do you find places like this?" Hilda said. "Much as I enjoy being the best-dressed woman here, I—"

"Modesty, woman, modesty."

"Rafferty, I'm the only woman wearing a skirt!"

"That may be so, but I find many of the T-shirt slogans have great social relevance."

———

We went to my house. "Burping gently into the good night," Hilda called it with post-pizza accuracy.

We put a bowl of milk on the back step but never saw the cat. The bowl was empty in the morning, though, when Ed and Ricco came around to haul me downtown.

"Wow," I said. "Can we turn on the siren?"

"This ain't funny," Ricco said. "This ain't funny at all."

13

We rode downtown in a department Dodge. Ricco drove. Ed sat up front with him, turned halfway around to talk to me. I had the backseat to myself.

This was not an especially good deal. You need a bad head cold or a clothespin to enjoy the backseat of a working police car.

"The Scotsmen want to talk to you," Ed said.

"I guess I came in late. What Scotsmen?"

"The klutzes who screwed all this up. It's a special antidrug group."

"A task force, no less," Ricco said. He sounded bitter.

Ed said, "Move Against Crack Task Force. MACTF. MacTuff. They call themselves The Scotsmen."

Ricco spat out the car window. "That bullshit name is one of them incentive gimmicks. You know, Tiger team and Eagle squad, all that motivational shit."

"What happened to just catching the bad guys?"

"It's hard to find time these days," Ed said.

Ricco said, "They got my goddamned incentive so high, I keep bumping into it."

A block later, I said, "These Scotsmen, they're the guys who wouldn't let anyone near the Mini-Maxi place; then they didn't show up themselves, right?"

"Yeah," Ed said.

"Why?"

"I want to hear Kevin's answer to that one myself," he said.

Ricco grunted cynically and spat out the window again.

"Kevin who?" I said. "Isn't this fun, guys, we're playing Twenty Questions during our ride in a real police car. Oh, boy, oh, boy, oh, boy."

Ricco found a pothole; Ed's jowls bounced. "I see your point," he said. "Okay. Kevin Noonebury runs this MacTuff thing. He conned a deputy chief into setting it up. I don't think you know Kevin. He's a lieutenant, but way up the list. A show-boater. Talks to civic groups; wears Italian suits; got a skinny wife with too many teeth. You know the type."

I said, "And late at night he hears small voices whispering, 'Chief Noonebury' in his shell-like ear."

"You got that right. Kevin'll probably make it, too. He's no more aggressive than your average mama grizzly defending her cubs."

I said, "You know, as a name, MacTuff sucks."

"Don't it?" Ricco said. "Sounds like a hamburger to me."

"Or a computer."

Ed said, "That's how they got involved with this Mini-Maxi thing. They must have a trigger on the computer. You phoned me about the possible hit, we did a routine scan on the address, and ten minutes later one of Noonebury's stooges told us to butt out."

I said, "To repeat myself, why?"

Ed scowled. "Let's see what Noonebury says."

"How big is this group of his? Sounds like they've got a lot of clout."

"Aw, the clout is because they're after crack. Half of what the TV and newspapers say about crack is bullshit, but the public doesn't know that. People are uptight about crack, which means the brass is uptight about crack."

Ricco said, "Which means Noonebury can do no fucking wrong." He cut over in front of a pickup truck, braked abruptly, and hooked a right toward the central business district.

Ed said, "Kevin's a political son of a bitch. He's dragged in a bunch of outside drones to make his MacTuff empire look bigger. There are four or five state guys attached to it now. And the local Feebies drop in every couple of days; they stand around in their tailored suits and say things like 'liaising' and 'maximization of enforcement resources.' Your federal government in action, huh? Oh, yeah, and DEA sent down one of their jerk-offs."

"Wonderful," I said. "And has this concentration of super-heroes accomplished anything yet?"

"A little bit, I guess. They've busted a bunch of street deal-ers. And a crack house or two. All low-level stuff, though."

"They're all arrest numbers," Ricco said. "Noonebury gets off on arrest numbers."

Ed rubbed his stomach and winced. "That's right," he said "Guys like us—you, me, Ricco—we think of the street. Who's the bad guy this time? how are we going to catch him? and so on. Noonebury thinks of computer printouts and bar graphs and percentages." He shook his head. "The man's a goddamned bean counter, Rafferty. He should be a CPA, not a cop."

We turned the corner around the DPD headquarters

building and dropped down the ramp into the underground garage. Ricco parked; we got out.

I said, "I'm disappointed in you, Ed. You're about to throw me into a room with a number dumper named Noonebury and a DEA dude in a Captain Drugbuster suit. This could seriously affect our friendship."

"Oh, I'm going in with you," he said. "I wouldn't miss this for anything."

"That's different," I said. "Can we hold hands if I get too scared?"

14

Kevin Noonebury was five-tennish, with short black hair, tiny white teeth, and a suit worth more than my car. He bustled Ed and me into a conference room—Ricco hadn't made the cut—and introduced the DEA rep. His name was Ernie Boyle. Or maybe it was Bailey; something like that.

We all sat down around a blond table. There were legal pads in front of Noonebury and Ernie Whosis, and a cassette tape recorder in the center of the table.

Noonebury sat very erect in his chair, pink-cheeked and after-shaved and perfect. He gave Ed and me two seconds of formal smile, punched a button on the tape recorder, and began to recite the date and time into it.

I pulled the recorder toward me and fiddled with it until it came open. Noonebury's eyes narrowed; Ernie's eyes widened and darted toward the closed door when I removed the tape, threw it and the recorder into opposite corners of the room, and leaned back in my chair. I smiled at Noonebury.

He didn't smile back. He said, "That was entirely uncalled

for." He probably used the same tone of voice when his kids left their bikes in the driveway.

"But it felt so good," I said. "And you don't really want a tape of me calling you a horse's ass. You know how those things get copied and passed around the department."

Noonebury leaned forward on his elbows and played with his felt-tip pen. He gave Ed a cold look.

Ed shifted in his chair; it creaked. "I'll take him out and pistol-whip him, Kevin, if it'll make you feel any better."

I said to Ed, "Watch what you say in front of old Ern here. He looks like those wimps who used to turn guys in for smoking in the locker room."

Ernie began to write things on his legal pad. He wrote very diligently. Without looking up, he said, "You do know you could be arrested for interfering with a police investigation, don't you?"

Noonebury looked pained. Ed rolled his eyes. I said, "Oh, no, Mistah Fox, don't throw Brer Rabbit in dat bad ole jail. 'Cause den he got to tell all dem lawyers and newspaper folks 'bout how da po-lice let dat poor man get kilt—"

"All right!" Noonebury snapped. "Could we attempt to conduct a little business here, please?"

"Good idea," I said. "All this power-play horseshit is boring." I smiled at him again. "How may I help you?"

Noonebury sighed. He said formally, "We are very interested in Carl Dresden and Max Krandorff, the principals of the Mini-Maxi Food Barn firm."

"Why?"

"I would prefer to hear your observations first. That way you won't subconsciously stress or diminish anything because of what you think I want to hear."

It was a valid point. Maybe Noonebury was a better cop than he looked. I told him about the day Dresden approached me downtown, the index card and my phone call to Ed the following morning.

Noonebury found a tight little smile somewhere and showed it to me. "You waited until the next day?"

"Yeah, I'm getting less and less happy about that myself."

Noonebury looked at Ed. "Prints?"

Ed shook his head. "Off sweaty paper? The lab guys laughed at me."

Noonebury said to me, "Were you or were you not specifically told to stay away from Krandorff and that location."

"Of course I was."

"But you didn't."

"Get knotted. Do you want information, or do you want to play power games again?"

Noonebury waved his hand angrily. Ernie from DEA looked disgusted. He probably wanted to do something really bad to me. Soap my car windows, maybe.

I told Noonebury about finding Max's body. I lied to him some. I told him I'd phoned Ed immediately, and I didn't tell him how I thought the hit had gone down. They had the body; let them work it out for themselves.

Noonebury wasn't too interested in that part anyway, but he wanted to know everything about Dresden when he showed up with the money. I told him the truth about that.

"How much money was in the case?" Noonebury said. "When you first got it."

"Twelve million dollars," I said. "I kept most of it to pay the phone bill."

Noonebury looked pained. Ed rumbled, "Don't get cute, Kevin. Check the goddamned case out of Property and count it yourself."

"I meant—"

"We know what you meant," Ed said.

"What is he, Ed," I said, "some kind of robot Internal Affairs built in their garage on the weekend?"

Noonebury's cheeks were even more pink now. He pointed a perfectly manicured finger at Ed. "You had orders, too, Durkee," he said. "We'll talk about that later."

Ed yawned at him. Ed must have found a deputy chief of his own.

I had to repeat everything I'd just told Noonebury and Ernie because cops don't believe even a phone number until you've said it three times.

Then they had a question or thirty. An hour and a half after we'd walked into the room, they were finally finished. I was hoarse. The room was stuffy. The DEA guy was sweating some, and even Ed looked more rumpled than usual. Kevin Noonebury was still ready for the cover of *GQ*.

"Now, Kevin," Ed said. "Why is that store so important to you?"

Ernie DEA frowned. Noonebury looked at me and frowned, too. "Let's get together later, Ed."

I said, "Doesn't matter. I hypnotize him, and he tells me everything."

Ed raised his hands, palms upward. "Happens all the time," he said. Maybe he had two deputy chiefs on his side.

Noonebury tightened his jaw momentarily, then nodded. "Very well. Our information is that the Mini-Maxi store is—or at least, was—being used as a crack warehouse."

Ed looked at me. I laughed.

Noonebury pressed his lips together and looked at the air between us. "We have a reliable informant."

"How reliable?" I said. "Did you find any crack in the store?"

Noonebury and Ernie thought about that a long time before Noonebury shook his head a quarter inch each way.

Ed scootched his chair closer to the table. He said, "Okay, Kevin, let's be realistic. You got diddled by a snitch. It's happened to all of us; it'll happen again. This is a murder case, not a drug case. So how about you let me have it back? That way you can concentrate your efforts on the drug aspect; run up the old arrest rate, eh? What do you say?" Ed smiled a great toothy, conciliatory smile; I was embarrassed for him.

Noonebury swiveled his eyes toward Ed like they were gun barrels. "The murder is part and parcel of the drug case. Associates fall out; they have each other killed regularly."

Ed dropped the smile. "Kevin, you're gonna fart around with this one, trying to make it what it isn't, and screw any chance of a conviction. If you haven't already. Did you really lock out the forensics team until after your people had turned over the whole goddamned store?"

Noonebury's eyes flickered with something—fright, embarrassment, anger—for a half second; then he had clamped down again. "It's my case, Ed. And I'm keeping it."

Ed sighed and stood up. "Come on, Rafferty."

Noonebury tilted his head to look up at Ed. "Have I said I'm finished with him?"

I said, "Underwear."

Noonebury frowned. "What did you say?"

"Underwear. Buy your underwear a size larger," I said. "That'll perk up that surly disposition."

Ed and I left and trudged back to his office. Ricco had gone somewhere; Ed checked out another car and drove me home. We didn't talk much on the way.

Ed stopped in front of my house and turned off the ignition. "So, what do you think of our boy, Kevin?"

"I recall a pungent saying about shit-house rats."

"Yeah. Uh, Rafferty, I'm gonna work on the Krandorff hit on the sly."

"Is it worth it, Ed? I mean, hell I can get away with things like that, but—"

"I've got a contact or two upstairs. Kevin can't—God, I hate this shit! Look, if you have any ideas, I'd appreciate them, okay?"

"Sure, Ed." I got out of the car.

"It's your fault, you know," Ed said. "You're a bad influence. Got me running around saving the world, for Christ's sake."

"Watch your back."

"Yeah. I'll call you." He tried a U-turn in the narrow street and had to back and fill twice to get the car around. When he was facing the right way, he took off, staring straight ahead with a frown on his big hound-dog face.

15

"This sucks," Ricco said. "How're you supposed to work a murder secondhand?" He took what had to be his sixth doughnut and dunked it into his coffee. "It's like getting laid with somebody else's dick."

I said to Ed Durkee, "Now there's a catchy phrase for you. Doubtless inspired by the gracious surroundings."

Ricco, Ed Durkee, and I sat in a park at an antique picnic table, not far from a fancy gazebo. All the bits and pieces were period items, from the signs to the cast-iron streetlight columns. I loved it. I wished I had a pinch-back suit like the one Robert Preston wore in *The Music Man*. To salve my loss, I hummed my special arrangement of "Ya Got Trouble," for baritone and shower stall. *Trouble with a capital* T *and that rhymes with …*

Not far from where we sat, old houses dripped with timber gingerbread and glowed with fresh paint. When what passed for progress had ravaged the east side of Dallas, people of rare good sense had saved these houses, had moved them here, and restored them.

The tiny time-machine subdivision and adjoining park were peaceful, elegant, restrained.

Which made it the last place you'd expect to find two sneaky cops and a pushy private thug drinking take-out coffee, eating doughnuts out of a bag, and trying to work out why Max Krandorff had died like that.

Ed rumbled, "I don't understand the kneecapping and hand chopping." He slurped coffee. "Maybe we're missing the obvious; maybe it was a righteous robbery. Maybe they tortured him for the safe combination."

"Trust me," I said. "Max was already stacking shelves at the great supermarket in the sky when they did that. I saw him, remember?"

Ed and Ricco grunted. Kevin Noonebury was still claiming drug connections; he had locked everyone else out. Ed and Ricco had been directly ordered to stay out of the Mini-Maxi. They were not taking it well.

Ricco said, "I go along with Rafferty, Ed, because of the wallet and the cash register. If it was a robbery, they'd have grabbed the loose cash for sure."

I nodded. "There wasn't much cash, but—"

"Right," said Ricco, "so let's go with that. He passed up a good chance to fake a nice tame robbery. Why?"

"He's stupid," Ed said.

"It wouldn't matter if he was," I said. "Disguising the hit as a robbery was part of the job specification, according to Dresden. He told me; he must have told the other guy."

"The hitter forgot," Ed said. He had the sleepy, bored look he uses when he plays devil's advocate.

"Naw," Ricco said, "a guy don't make mistakes like that. He goes in the front door thinking: I'm gonna waste this dude and make it look like a robbery. He don't forget two minutes later, then shoot at knees just to kill time until he remembers why he's there."

"Colorful," I said, "and logical." I took the last doughnut out of the bag and split it with Ed. Ricco had out-eaten us two to one, but who counts? "How about this? The guy panicked?"

"That one don't fly, either. Takes just as much time and thought to shoot and chop as it does to grab the cash." Ricco looked at the empty doughnut bag, then picked up his coffee. He started to drink, then stopped suddenly. "And besides, if he changed his mind at the last minute, where did the goddamned ax come from?"

Ed said, "You got me. Before we get too far down the cover-up trail, let's work on why Dresden wanted Krandorff taken out in the first place."

I said, "Money. Dresden said he needed the insurance payout from their keyman policy."

"When my baby goes to Rio," Ricco sang off-key. Which was bad enough, but then he added, "doo-dah, doo-dah," at the end.

"I don't think so," I said. "My impression was that Dresden intended the money to go into the company. He said they were about to go under."

Ed said, "Why were they going under?"

Ricco said, "Stop me if you've heard this one. Max had his hand in the till."

"Probably," I said. "And Dresden figured to replace what Max had stolen with the insurance money."

"Don't forget, Dresden would have been royally pissed off, too," Ricco said. "A little revenge goes a long way."

I said, "Dresden didn't seem angry. He seemed more reluctant, even resigned. He acted like having Max hit was something he didn't want to do, but he felt it was necessary. A chore."

"Taking out the garbage," Ed said.

"Washing dishes," Ricco said.

"And—I'd forgotten this—he asked me if there was a way to kill Max without hurting him."

Ricco looked thoughtful. "Tell you what, that's interesting. I bet a quick one in the back of the head is the most painless way out. You ain't around long enough for it to hurt."

Ed grunted. "Waiting for it wouldn't be much fun, though."

We all thought about that awhile; then I said, "Maybe he told the other guy how to shoot Max. He didn't tell me."

"There's another thing," Ed said. "I thought Krandorff wasn't supposed to be hit until tonight. What happened there?"

I looked at the dregs of cold coffee in the bottom of my cup. "I'm not too happy about that, either, Ed. If I'd gone straight to the store instead of sitting around convincing Hilda what a stouthearted crusader I am, Max would—"

"Bullshit," Ricco said. "If you're going to start that, you gotta put Ed and me on the list, too."

After a few moments I said, "They talked on the phone Tuesday night. Maybe the hitter called Dresden to see why he hadn't showed up that day; maybe Dresden called the hitter for some reason. However it happened, it must have been a weird conversation. Dresden thought he was talking to me, and I was using a code in case someone was listening."

Ricco said, "This Dresden guy. Can he really walk and talk and dress himself like a grown-up?"

"There's some doubt in my mind," I said.

"No shit." Ricco shook his head. "This dropkick owns

three stores, and I'm busting my guts as a wage slave? It ain't fair."

I said to Ed, "During the call they must have changed the day from Thursday to Wednesday, but I don't know why."

Ed chewed his lip, then said, "Maybe the hitter realized it was coming unraveled. He wanted to go ahead before it was too late."

"Guy's got big balls to look at it that way," Ricco said. "Most of the half-assed hitters around here would cancel out if they thought the target had a spare crutch to throw at them."

I said, "Maybe the work schedule at the store changed. Someone called in sick or needed a night off, so Max was going to be there last night but not tonight. It could be that simple."

Ed took the empty doughnut bag and smoothed it on the table-top. "It could be even simpler. Maybe the hit was a day early because this wasn't the real hit."

Ricco and I shook our heads. "Aw, c'mon, Ed," Ricco said. "We already did that number."

Ed said, "Hey, I agree with you. No robbery. But how about kids? Juiced-up, maybe, or flying high and mean on who knows what. A dare. One of them says, 'Bet you won't go in there and do the old man.' 'Will, too.' Can't you see a couple of stoned kids doing that?"

I said, "Maybe ..."

Ricco said, "No way. Kids would take the wallet, whether that's why they went in there or not. They love that bank plastic. Little fuckers have been raised on automatic teller machines; they can play 'em like pinball games."

"Okay," Ed said. A good devil's advocate never takes defeat too seriously, He said, "Let's work on the basis that Dresden's hit man did the job and tried to disguise it. You figure they changed the cover-up from robbery to psycho the same time they changed the day?"

"Probably," I said.

Ricco shrugged. "Listen," he said, "as a cover, this psycho-killing gimmick don't work at all for me."

Ed said, "No. He didn't know enough to use multiple wounds. One lousy cut means no psycho to me."

Ricco said, "Funny thing, though. I worked a one-cut psycho killing once. This loony-tunes thought his neighbor was a Martian stud or something, so he decided to castrate him. To save earth-women, see? Anyway, he used his hedge clippers and the guy bled to death. That was only one cut. But, yeah, Ed, you're right. The psycho angle here is a scam."

A young couple with two small children strolled into the park. The kids ran, whooping, for the gazebo and began to play peek-a-boo through the fancy timberwork. Mom and Dad stood fifty from our picnic table and chatted. Mom had her back to us. And a very nice back it was, too.

"So where are we?" I said.

Ed shrugged a few more rumples into his suit. "Stuck, for the moment. We can't think of anyone except Dresden's hitter who might have clipped Krandorff. Not that it ..." Ed's armpit chirped. He switched his beeper off.

Ricco said, "That'll be Kevin Noonebury calling, Ed. Just in case you were somewhere having a good time."

They stood up. Ricco headed for their car at the curb; Ed put the empty cups into the bag and looked around for a trash can.

"What about Dresden?" I said.

"What about him? His secretary says he's in Houston on business. At a Holiday Inn. The Holiday Inn says that, too. They haven't exactly seen him since noon Thursday, but he must still be there because he hasn't checked out. Hotel logic.

A friend of mine on the force down there is going to look around." Ed handed me the bag of garbage. "Here, for Christ's sake. I bought it, and Ricco ate most of it. Least you can do is throw the scraps away."

———

Ten minutes later, two miles away, I realized I'd had the same white Ford Tempo in the mirror for too long. I made four consecutive right turns; the Tempo stayed with me all the way around the block. Damn! That son of a bitch Noonebury!

l knew the Tempo had not tailed me to the park, but it might have found us there. Or maybe Noonebury's stooges had picked me up just now. I hoped so. Ed and Ricco deserved at least a few days before they had to pry nosy Scotsmen off their backs.

I pulled over to the curb and stopped. The Tempo coasted past. The driver was alone in the car, and he turned away as he went past. I think he had a mustache.

I waited until other cars had passed, then pulled out. Two blocks farther on, with the Tempo a block ahead of me I made a dozen random lefts and rights, then headed away at a right angle to my original direction. I didn't see the Tempo after that.

16

"Pâté?" I said.

Hilda looked wary. "That depends. Is it the real stuff? Honest-to-God liver pâté? Or is it that gunk you make from sardines and cream cheese?"

I said, "Hundreds of geese remain in mourning. Film at ten."

She beamed a zillion-watt smile at me. "I'd love some, thank you."

Sunday afternoon. My backyard. I had talked myself out of trimming the bushes for another week, persuasive devil that I am. Hilda and I were either taking our ease in the garden or loafing, depending on your background and pretensions.

We'd almost finished the newspapers heaped on an outdoor table between our lawn chairs. There was a tub of ice, beer, and chardonnay nearby. The barbecue was ten minutes from ready for two giant T-bones. We had laughed a lot in the past few hours, and winked at each other, and decided there might be better ways to spend the day, but offhand, we couldn't think of any.

Hilda's scurrilous slander of my famous sardine pâté made me remember I still had a little bit left over somewhere in the back of the refrigerator. When I went inside for the real stuff I got the sardine mixture, too, and put that bowl on the ground near the fence.

Hilda smiled. "Are you still trying to catch that cat?"

"I don't want to catch it. It drops by sometimes, I offer it a snack, that's all. Hostwise I am a very generous guy."

"Hostwise you're a soft touch. That's someone's pet, Rafferty. If you want a cat, go buy one. Or ask around; people are always trying to give away kittens."

"Is this a female nesting urge or something? A man slips a passing cat a quick snack, and zap! You're pushing me into the zoo business."

Hilda grinned. "My mistake. It's obvious the cat means absolutely nothing to you." In the house the phone rang.

I got up and started for the back door. "What cat?" I said.

"Exactly," Hilda said. "And now your phone is ringing. I find the timing suspiciously opportune."

"Cat people stick together, cookie," I said from the doorway. Hilda made a face at me as I reached in for the wall phone. "Hello."

A man's voice said, "Rafferty?" The voice was almost familiar. "Is this Rafferty?" he said again, and I recognized him. It was the turkey who'd called me at the office last Thursday.

"I believe Mr. Rafferty is in the card room," I said. "I'll have him paged."

"What? Hey, come on! Cut the crap." He sounded menacing, but he also sounded like he was working at it. "You've got something I want."

"Charm?" I said. "Grace under pressure? A dynamite profile?"

"What's with you? You can't even talk—aw, shit!" He banged the phone down. Hard.

I hung up, too, and walked back to Hilda. She looked up from the features section. "What was that all about?"

"Guy doesn't know what a t'gallant is, and it's bugging the hell out of him."

"Perhaps you'd care to explain that," Hilda said.

"Certainly. T'gallant; a contraction of topgallant; one of the sails on a square-rigged ship. I looked it up."

"Rafferty ..." She gave me that look. I told her about the other phone call while I poked at the coals in the barbecue.

Hilda thought about it while I went to the kitchen for the steaks. When I came back, she was frowning. "He called your office Thursday and here today," she said. "Do you suppose it has anything to do with that convenience store fiasco?"

I was searing steaks and dodging smoke when she said that and I didn't give it enough thought.

"It's that yellow pages ad," I said. "I think I'll change it next year. This one pulls too many weirdos out of woodwork."

So I cooked the steaks, and Hilda put dressing on her salad and we dined, and we lazed away the rest of the afternoon and evening. The mood ranged somewhere between great and wonderful, as days spent with Hilda tended to do.

It was only much later, in the dark quiet night hours, that I found out how wrong I was.

17

The firebomb came through the open bedroom window and landed on Hilda's legs.

I was barely awake, returning from the bathroom, when it happened. Hilda said "Ouch!" in a muzzy, aggrieved tone. Then she opened one eye and saw the burning rag in the bottle's neck. She screamed, scrabbled up to cower against the head of the bed and kicked out frantically at the flaming bottle.

So far only the rag fuse was aflame; the bottle had not broken and dumped out the gasoline inside. I dived onto the bed and grabbed for the bottle, trying to catch it before Hilda kicked it against something hard and turned herself into a bonfire.

I didn't do very well; I had the bottle briefly, I dropped it, snagged it on the fly when Hilda kicked it, then bobbled and fumbled and banged it against the footboard with a clang that terrified me.

I felt like a bit player in a bad puppet show; clumsy and out of touch. I could hear myself grunt in frustration as I fumbled with the elusive bottle.

The gasoline-soaked rag fuse was burning with smoky, fierce flames a foot high. Once the rag slapped against the back of my right hand. There was a brief wet sensation, then strangely cool fire and the stench of singed hair.

I don't know how long my hand was on fire. The next time I looked, the flame had gone out by itself.

And while I juggled the potential fireball around the bed I wondered when another one would come sailing into the bedroom. Or was this a diversion, and the real attack was still to come? How close would they get? Backyard close or leaning-in-the-window close? Handguns, shotguns, or automatic weapons?

Bobbling and burning and fumbling and trying to think. Oh, Christ, Hilda, sweetheart, please stop screaming so I can hear them if they come. And get out of the bed. Are they still outside? Come *here*, bottle, and, Hilda, hit the floor before …

And then, finally, I had a decent grip on the goddamned thing. I lurched into the bathroom; I must have banged my knee on the bed or something. I burned my hand again when I pulled the fuse out and threw it into the shower stall. Carefully, I put the bottle into the bathroom sink, then stumbled out to the hall closet for my shotgun.

When I returned to the bedroom, I was armed and beginning to get on top of the situation. The bedside clock blinked 2:17 at me in large red letters. I remembered seeing 2:13 when I had climbed out of bed to go to the bathroom.

Hilda had stopped screaming now. She sat at the head of the bed, her knees drawn up and her arms wrapped tightly around them. Her breathing was loud and raspy, with a quiver of near-hysteria each time she inhaled.

"It's okay, babe," I said, and went to the window.

Outside, the yard was quiet and apparently empty. The attacker—attackers?—might be hiding in the bushes, of course, but at least they weren't about to come through the window right then.

I went to Hilda. "Come on, Hil. It's all over now. No problem." I babbled platitudes to her and tugged her arm. Slowly she unfolded and let me lead her to the bathroom. It was no fort, but it was the closest room that did not have an external wall.

Hilda clutched my arm with a hand like a claw. She didn't speak, though her breathing seemed a little better. Only a little, though. When we got to the bathroom, she saw the still-burning fuse on the floor of the shower and wailed a high, thin sound that cut right through me.

Hilda sank slowly to the floor. I patted her shoulder clumsily. She twitched like a startled animal. "I'll fix it, Hil. Don't worry. I'll fix it."

I turned the shower on to put out the flaming rag and held my burned hand under the cool water. It helped some.

"I'm sorry, Hil. It's okay now, really. Just stay here for a minute. I'll be right back."

I found my big flashlight and went hunting.

Out the front door and carefully around the house, staying close to the fence. Whoever had thrown the firebomb was probably long gone now, but I couldn't count on that.

The straggly bushes I had cheerfully neglected were a problem now; it took twenty careful minutes to be certain the yard was empty. I found where he had lighted the fuse. There were three burnt paper matches on the ground near a bois d'arc tree. A clue. Big deal.

I checked the street. There were five cars parked on the short street. All five were familiar and empty. There were no house lights, except for mine, and even the neighborhood Irish setter had taken the night off.

I was losing my adrenaline energy; feeling the jangly

downside of the buzz. My mouth tasted sour and metallic. My burned hand hurt, and my knee had stiffened up.

And I suddenly realized I was standing in the middle of a suburban street, stark naked, holding a shotgun.

I went inside.

Hilda was in the bedroom again, sitting dejectedly on the side of the bed. The bed had been stripped; only the bare mattress and pillows remained. She gestured vaguely. "The covers were smoldering. I put them in the shower."

"How are you, babe?"

She sighed and tried to smile. "Okay, I guess. Scared. Embarrassed, a little."

I said, "Don't be."

"I really screamed, didn't I?"

"Really did. It's okay."

There was a half inch of water on the bathroom floor. A smoke-stained pile of bedding filled the overflowing shower base. I turned off the shower and dragged the bedding clear of the drain.

The firebomb bottle was still in the sink. Better find a cap for that, or put it in the garage. Or pour it out.

Then, I realized it didn't smell. Even the bottle's neck had only a small whiff of gasoline. Strange. But didn't they mix detergent with the gasoline? Maybe that would mask the smell. I poured some into the palm of my good hand. It didn't look like gasoline, or detergent, or a combination of the two. I smelled the puddle. Nothing. I tasted it.

Well, goddamn.

Back in the bedroom, I sat beside Hilda on the edge of the bed and showed her the bottle. "Look at this. A champagne bottle. Big, heavy, and hard to break; kind of dumb, when it's supposed to shatter and splash burning gasoline all over the place."

Hilda shuddered and looked away. "Is that bottle a clue?" She said it in a who-cares tone of voice.

"I doubt it. Probably swiped from a restaurant garbage can. Anyway, the next part is the most interesting." I tipped up the bottle, sipped, and handed it to her.

"Rafferty! Gasoline will ..." Then she sniffed the bottle. "Water?"

"Yep. Apparently I did my three-handed shortstop routine for nothing."

Hilda looked anxious. "I don't understand this. I don't understand any of this."

"It was supposed to be a warning, I think."

"A warning of what?"

I shrugged. "I'm not sure."

"Well, then, a warning from who?"

I shrugged again. "Can't tell yet."

"Now I'm really scared," Hilda said. "This is—"

The telephone beside the bed rang. I picked it up. "Go ahead," I said.

It was the man who had called before. He said, "You smart-ass, are you gonna listen to me, now?

"What do you mean, *now*?"

"No more fucking around, Rafferty. Next time I'll put gasoline in it. Think about that."

"I will," I said, "among other things. So what's on your mind?"

His voice climbed a tone. "What the fuck do you *think* is on my mind? That dumb son of a bitch gave you my money. I want it."

I felt like little kids must feel when they finally realize there's no Santa Claus. Suddenly everything made sense. I was ashamed that I'd been so blindly, stubbornly dumb.

"You did the Krandorff hit," I said.

"What?"

"The grocery store guy. Max."

"Never you mind about that. You just worry about getting me my money."

"What makes you think I—"

"I saw you!" He half screamed it. "I told you to stop trying to fuck around with me!"

"Okay," I said, "calm down. I have the money right here. Come on over."

"Oh, that's cute. As if I'm gonna—"

"Pick a time and place, then. I'll meet you."

"Yeah …" He sounded suddenly wary. "I'll call you. Be available."

"Sure."

He hung up then. So did I.

As if the phone was a switch, Hilda jumped up and began to dress. "Rafferty, I want to get out of here. Now!"

"I don't blame you, babe."

I kept the shotgun on the backseat while I drove Hilda home. Just in case. On the way, I explained that the hit man didn't know about her.

"He barely knows about me," I said. "Looks like he whacked Max; then later on he saw Dresden give me the money. He spotted my license number and got my name from that."

Hilda sounded doubtful. "I thought only the police could do that."

"Yeah, some cops think that, too."

We drove in silence for a while. "Hil, honey, I'm sorry about this. If I'd paid attention, if I hadn't teased the guy on the phone—"

She put her hand on my leg. "It's not your fault. I'll be all right. Just … give me a little time. Please."

"Sure."

We got to Hilda's house a few minutes before four. The back of my hand had bubbled up in fat, squishy blisters. Hilda bandaged it. She frowned when I asked her not to put any tape on my trigger finger.

Hilda looked to see why her shoes hurt and found she'd been burned, too. There were dime-size blisters on her feet and ankles.

I put bandages on Hilda's blisters, fed her more brandy than she wanted, and put her to bed. I sat on the bed with her. At first she kept opening her eyes to look at me. Then she fell asleep and burbled softly.

I dozed off, too, and slipped into a nightmare where it happened again, except this time the bottle broke, and there was burning gasoline everywhere, and Hilda was—

I came up out of it with my heart pounding, clammy with fear until I saw Hilda sleeping peacefully beside me. It took me a long time to calm down.

After that I wandered around her house, not carrying the shotgun, but keeping it handy. A little before six I made coffee, drank a cup, leaning against the kitchen counter, but the caffeine reacted with the old adrenaline and made me jumpy.

At seven o'clock I called Cowboy.

18

owboy and Mimi arrived two hours later in a red, open Jeep that squeaked to a stop four inches from Hilda's garage door. Cowboy unfolded his lanky frame from the passenger seat and stood beside the dusty Jeep. He shook his head, took off his big western hat, and slapped it against the leg of his jeans. And he grumbled.

"Woman drives this thang like a herd bull with a gut ache," he said. "Skitterin' all over creation lookin' fer somethin' to fight with."

Mimi sat behind the wheel with a grin on her wide face. "How-do, Rafferty. You like my new play-pretty?" She proudly waved her arm at the Jeep.

I clucked my tongue and whistled and said, "Now *that's* a Jeep!"

"No extra cushions," she said, and bounced happily. The driver's seat had been modified so she could reach the pedals. Let's face it; Mimi is short.

Make that *very* short.

Cowboy settled his hat onto his head and tugged it down to rest exactly half an inch above his eyebrows. He insists he didn't get that gesture from James Coburn in *The Magnificent Seven*, but I still wonder. They could be twins.

"Mimi wanted her a car that fit," Cowboy said. "And the Little Rock job paid us a right nice bonus, so we figgered it was time." He pronounced it "tahm."

"What Little Rock job?" I said.

Cowboy lifted two soft sports bags out of the open space behind the Jeep's seats. "Couple of no-goods was trying to chase off one of them big chicken farmers up that-a-way. Wanted his land, I guess. They kept burning his sheds, anyway. He lost him a whole bunch of birds."

"I assumed you reasoned with the miscreants and returned them to the path of rectitude."

"Naw," Cowboy said, "we kicked their butts instead."

Mimi giggled. "You sure can talk that fancy trash Rafferty."

I said, "Sounds like it was fairly quick and easy."

Cowboy hefted the bags and walked toward the house. "Yeah, I guess it was at that. We only had to shoot the one of 'em."

———

When I checked on Hilda, she was still asleep, sprawled on her back with one leg outside the bedcovers. That position, and the bandages on her exposed foot, gave her a disturbingly vulnerable air. I had a sudden flash of her sleeping in my bed last night just before the firebomb came through the window. My chest felt hollow as I closed her bedroom door.

In the kitchen Cowboy and Mimi sat on stools with their hands around coffee mugs. I offered them breakfast; they had already eaten.

"Tell us 'bout the opposition," Cowboy said.

"That won't take very long. So far, he's only a voice on the phone."

But it took the best part of an hour to fill in the background of Mini-Maxi Food Barns, Carl Dresden and Max Krandorff, Kevin Noonebury's Scotsmen, and, finally, last night's attack.

While I talked, I made toast, smeared it with peanut butter and ate. I offered to share, but they still weren't hungry.

"I'll give you a double helping of peanut butter," I said, "if you want it to stick to the roof of your mouth en mak ya tok fahnny."

Mimi shook her head. "Like a big kid, I swear," she said.

Cowboy poured himself another half cup of coffee. "On the phone you said we was gonna split up."

"Right. I want Mimi to stay with Hilda while you and I go find the guy."

Cowboy said, "Sure." Mimi nodded.

I said, "Tell you the truth, I don't think he even knew Hilda was there last night. And he doesn't have a beef with her. But even so …"

"Question," Mimi said. "Are we talking about a siege? You want us to really hunker down and hide?"

"No. Hilda wouldn't stand for that, and it shouldn't be necessary. Once Cowboy and I leave here, we'll stay away so the hitter can't backtrack through us." I thought about that for a minute, then added, "Well, we won't come back until we work out a decent cutout, anyway. Maybe a rental car and a secure changeover point somewhere; I don't know yet."

"Fine," she said. "We won't have any problems."

"Stick with her, Mimi. Stick close."

She nodded again.

I said, "You'll like hanging around Hilda's store. Lots of neat old stuff in there."

Mimi grinned at Cowboy. "Neat old stuff everywhere you look these days."

Cowboy smiled at her, reached out, and gently ran one knobby knuckle down her jawline. Mimi damn near purred.

I went to wake up Hilda.

———

"Rafferty, I'll feel foolish, having a bodyguard, but ... thank you." Hilda leaned against her pillow, bright and alert, even though she had been awake for less than three minutes. It amazes me. She can even eat breakfast as soon as she opens her eyes. I don't understand it.

"Mimi doesn't look like a bodyguard," I said. "You can tell people she's your little sister from Abilene. Just don't expect her to follow you through any metal detectors."

Hilda nodded. After a moment she said, "I dreamed about last night. In the dream the bottle was burning us. We were going to die."

"But that didn't happen, Hil, and it won't. How are you this morning?"

"All right, I think. It was only a dream. I know that." Firm voice, chin up, eyes front. "I can handle it."

"Way to go, babe. I'll find the guy, and while I'm doing that, you'll be okay with Mimi."

"She is good at this sort of thing, isn't she?" Hilda sounded thoughtful, not worried.

"Oh, yeah. I'm a little better; so is Cowboy. Mostly that's because of our size. We're stronger; we can hit harder and use larger weapons than Mimi. But she's very good. I'd trust her to cover my back anytime."

"Quite a recommendation."

I looked at her. "If Mimi wasn't that good, I couldn't leave you with her, Hil."

She blinked rapidly. "Damn. You did it again. I think you're talking about some dumb macho thing, then it turns out to be sentimental."

I said, "Roses are red, violets are blue, I'd beat up a mugger, to show I love you."

Hilda rolled her eyes. "Hallmark, eat your heart out," she said.

"I got a million of 'em."

"Spare me, please," she said, and swung her legs out of bed. "Go put a danish in the oven, will you? I'm starving!"

See what I mean about early morning food?

———

Before Cowboy and I left Hilda's house, I phoned Ed Durkee at the cop shop and told him what had happened.

"Is she all right?" he said.

"Couple of blisters. Bad dreams. Overall, though, she's doing pretty well."

Ed grunted. "What can I do? Assuming Noonebury doesn't get my badge lifted in the next twenty minutes, of course."

"Is it that bad, Ed?"

"No, not really. Hell, I might even be making a little progress. We'll see. Again, what can I do?"

"Saturday, after we split up at the park, a White Ford Tempo tailed me. He wasn't at the park; I'm pretty sure he picked me up afterward. I didn't bother to get the plate number, because I figured it was only one of Noonebury's drones. But now I wonder if it might have been Dresden's hired hitter."

"Hmm. Well, I know the Scotsmen have more cars than you can count. And they're paying expenses for some guys to use their own wheels. Street people can spot the unmarked departmental units faster than I can. So—look, I'll get started now. You come on in here. Depending on what I find out, we'll go give Kevin a hard time, or see what Motor Registration has to say." He paused, then said, "Do you need a backup? Because I could maybe find a squad for a day—"

"Thanks, Ed. It's okay. Cowboy and Mimi are—"

"Oh shit. Don't tell me things like that, Rafferty!" He hung up.

Hilda and I changed each other's bandages. Her feet didn't look too bad. My hand looked terrible, but the blisters hadn't broken. And it didn't hurt too much.

Cowboy loaded his sports bag and a canvas duffel bag heavy with weapons into my Mustang. We checked Hilda's neighborhood for three blocks in each direction. There was no one sitting and watching the house, so we headed south.

For the next thirty minutes, we crisscrossed our path, stopped on one-way streets, and doubled back half a dozen times. For our finale Cowboy stood on a street corner to see who, if anyone, followed me around the block. Twice.

No one did. *Nada*. We had come away from Hilda's without leaving a trail. Which was good, in one way, but bad in another. It would have been so much easier if he'd been there.

"We could have plucked him off our tail like a duck eating June bugs," Cowboy said.

"Life's a bitch," I said, "and then you come up with corn pone expressions like that."

Cowboy squirmed down in his seat and propped one knee

against the dash. "Let's stop driving, boss-man," he said. "If this dude is gonna phone to set up a meet, we're purely making life hard for that old boy."

"Soon. First let's go see what Ed Durkee came up with."

Cowboy humphed. "If it's all the same to you. I'll wait in the car."

"Good idea. That way no one will try to steal it."

Cowboy looked out at the Mustang's faded hood and ran his hand over my duct-tape-patched upholstery. "I don't think you need to worry too much about that," he said.

19

Ed Durkee came out of his office as I approached it. "Come on," he said. "Let's go see Noonebury."

"What've you got, Ed? Was the Tempo one of his?"

"I doubt it. Let's go pull his chain anyway."

————

Up in the rarefied mists of MacTuff land, they were questioning a thin black kid. The kid wore designer jeans, a gold watch, and top-of-the-line Reeboks. He kept his chin down and his eyes on the Reeboks. He answered every question with a shrug or a "nunh." He was twelve years old; thirteen, tops.

The cop asking the questions was slender, too, with a small dark mustache and sad eyes. His ID said his name was Frigerio. He didn't seem to mind that he didn't get any answers. He kept plugging along anyway, asking trick questions like "What's your name?" and "Where do you live?"

Frigerio looked like one of those people who never sweat.

Maybe that was in the job description for MacTuff appointments.

Kevin Noonebury stood behind Frigerio. Noonebury was shirtsleeved but immaculate. He had one hand on his hip. He used the other hand to tap a manicured forefinger against his pursed lips.

Noonebury saw Ed and me. He shifted the busy forefinger to a brief give-me-a-minute gesture.

Frigerio asked the kid, "Where did you get the car?"

The kid shrugged and said "nunh" again.

Someone stepped over and showed Noonebury a sheet of paper. He looked at it, handed it back, and watched Frigerio again. After five more minutes Noonebury turned away and walked to an empty corner of the large room. Ed and I followed him.

Noonebury said softly, "This is the sort of thing I'm up against every day, Ed. An hour ago, a Cadillac had a fender bender with a taxi. It was practically out front; only five or six blocks down Commerce. The Cadillac is brand new—something like seven hundred miles on it. That boy was driving it. He jumped out to run, tripped and fell flat on his face in front of an officer on foot patrol."

Noonebury glanced over his shoulder. Frigerio still placidly pitched questions, still sweatlessly struck out.

"See the boy's clothes and accessories?" Noonebury said. "He had almost eight hundred dollars in cash and a dozen crack packs in his pockets. The Cadillac is not on the hot sheet; my guess is it's his. And I suspect we'll find out he paid cash for it. Look at him. He's what, fourteen? Perhaps not even that old. Any minute now he'll remember to tell us his age. When he does, I'll have to ship him over to Youth. He'll get a reprimand, perhaps counseling, and then he'll go straight back to the crack dealer he works for. The current system doesn't work, Ed. The system says minors can't go to jail because they'll be exposed to criminals. So, on the streets, the drug dealers recruit children like that boy over there."

Noonebury gritted his perfect teeth and waggled a pointing finger. It was the closest I'd seen him come to passion. "Last week we found a runner who is ten, Ed. Ten years old, and he had more cash in his pocket than his father makes in a year."

Noonebury turned his hand palm up. He was selling now. "Ed, I want to get the people who use these children. If I have to spend hours in meetings soothing nervous deputy chiefs, it diminishes my effectiveness. Surely you can see that."

Ed sighed. "It diminishes *my* effectiveness when I can't work a murder case because you're hogging the file and evidence, Kevin. What about that white Tempo?"

Noonebury didn't like that, but he took it. Very interesting. Ed had definitely picked up some clout.

Noonebury seemed to force a pleasant expression onto his face. "One of my men has a red Tempo, but we're not using a white one. Of course, without the license number, it's difficult to ..." He spread his hands and smiled. "In any case, I assure you there is no current surveillance on Rafferty."

"That slight stress on the word *current* brings a question leaping to my fertile mind," I said.

Noonebury ignored me. He said to Ed, "I'm disturbed that you think I would put a tail on you and your sergeant, ah, Ricco. Very disturbed."

"Sure," Ed said. "Let's get together someday and talk about it."

"You could do lunch," I said. "Or take a meeting."

"Let's go, Rafferty."

As we passed Frigerio's desk, the kid suddenly lifted his

head and blurted, "Thirteen! I is thirteen years old, and I doan gotta talk to no honky cops!"

"Well, shit," said Frigerio.

———

When we got back to Ed's office, there was a portable cellular phone on his desk blotter. It was ringing. Well, it was beeping, or chirping; whatever you want to call that noise.

Ed picked up the handset, listened for a moment, then said, "Yeah. Okay, great. Thanks."

He hung up and handed me the portable phone. It was about the size of a telephone book and shaped a little like a briefcase, with the handset clipped onto the top. It was heavier than it looked.

"Here," he said. "You can't just sit around and wait for the hitter to call. You'll probably have to go find him. I've had a transfer patch put on your home phone. Any calls to it will be automatically switched to this thing."

"You're going out on a limb, Ed. I appreciate it."

He looked around his office and shrugged his rumpled shoulders. "Yeah, well, I guess I do owe a few favors now, but … Listen, Rafferty, if the hitter calls to set up the meet, I want to know. If you find him first, I want to know. And if you see or hear from Carl Dresden, I want to know that, too. You're getting a lot of slack because Kevin is busting my balls, but this is still my murder case."

I grimaced. "Ed, I can't have four hundred cops breathing down my neck, playing elaborate ambush games. I'm sorry, but—"

"What did I just say about Kevin? If I could get any help from real cops, would I use you?" He slapped futilely at the air between us. "Call me, goddamn it. We'll work it out."

Ed went to a file cabinet and grabbed an inch-high stack of computer printouts. "Take this, too." He dropped it on my side of his cluttered desk. "That's every white, beige, cream, and light yellow Tempo in North Texas. Damned if I know what good it will do you. Too many cars for you to track down alone and I can't get the manpower, so ..." He looked embarrassed.

"That's great, Ed," I said. "Thanks."

"Yeah, well, sometimes all this high-tech crap is actually useful. Good luck."

I gathered up my goodies and lugged them down to the parking lot. Cowboy sat on my front fender. In the next space, a tall redhead with long legs locked the door of a green Caprice.

"Hey," I said to Cowboy, "wait till you see this gadget."

Because sometimes things happen with perfect timing, the portable phone rang just as I plunked it down on the hood of the Mustang. Cowboy's eyebrows went up. The redhead turned around, a half smile on her face.

I said to Cowboy, "Ah, that will be Luther in Geneva about the takeover," and unclipped the phone handset. He nodded solemnly. The redhead slowly put her keys in her purse and watched me. Her head was cocked a little; she had nice eyes.

"This is Rafferty," I said to the phone.

It was Mrs. Jorgenson, my landlady. My last rent check had bounced.

Cowboy nearly hurt himself when he slipped off the fender, he was laughing so hard.

20

As we pulled out of the parking lot, Cowboy said, "I reckon we ought to get the money ready first. That way, if the hitter wants a meet real quick-like, we're all set to go."

"Fat chance of me giving that sucker fifteen thousand bucks."

"'Course not," Cowboy said patiently, "but it makes sense to take the money along. These setups never work out the way they should; you know that. Could be you'll need to show the cash early on, before we get to thumping on this old boy and any buddies he brings along. Don't sweat it, boss-man, we ain't gonna give away your money."

"You've got that right," I said. "I don't have the money. I turned it over to Ed Durkee."

Cowboy looked at me bleakly. Finally he took a deep breath and shook his head a little. "Gonna get you a hat before I let you stand out in the sun again."

We went to my office first. Maybe the hitter—it was annoying to know so little about him, not even a partial name—maybe the hitter thought I had stashed the money there. Maybe he'd already tried to steal it. Maybe.

And then again, maybe not. Beth Woodland said she hadn't noticed anyone hanging around. "What's the problem?"

"No problem. He's supposed to, uh, collect some money from me. I thought I might have missed him."

Beth frowned. "Since when are you looking for a bill collector instead of the other way around?"

Across the hall the aluminum-cookware sales manager had a different attitude. "Me, I figure it like this," he said. "Any bastard who can get money out of me, he's the best. So what I want to do is hire him and send him out after the dead-beats who owe *me*." He smiled around his cigar. "It ain't happened yet, though."

In my office, Cowboy sat slumped in my chair, his feet on my desk and his big hat pulled down over his eyes.

"You asleep?" I said.

"Can't stand to look at the mess," he said. "Now what?"

"Let's check the street again, in case he's watching the building. Then my house, for the same reason. After that I guess we punt."

Cowboy grunted. "Tell the kicker to suit up," he said. "Sure as hell, we gonna need him."

———

It was late afternoon as we approached my house on Palm Lane. It's a short street with only one way in or out. Cowboy and I circled in, checking surrounding blocks, turning left at every street corner.

"Mockingbird to Delmar to Ravendale to Matilda to Palm," I said. "Sounds like a double play sequence where they drop the ball a lot."

Cowboy grunted. "You really think we're gonna find this old boy sitting on your doorstep?"

"No. But I'd sure feel stupid if we pulled into the driveway, he hopped my fence and got away in his car parked on the next street."

"There is that," Cowboy said.

There were no Ford Tempos parked anywhere near Palm Lane, though, and no one pretended to wait for a bus or deliver a pizza or search for "Bill Brown's house." There was an elderly man I recognized walking a poodle, a departing UPS truck, and three women jogging.

As I stopped the Mustang in my driveway, I said, "And you don't think those were grenades in the last jogger's hip pockets?"

"Naw, that was all her. Probably why she jogs in the first place."

The house was empty and apparently untouched since Hilda and I had left in the dark hours of that morning.

"Damn," Cowboy said when he saw the bedroom and bath. "I knowed you wasn't much for housekeeping, but ..."

He examined the champagne bottle and charred fuse while I lugged dripping sheets to the washing machine. We mopped up the bathroom with towels, and threw those into the machine with the sheets. Cowboy got two beers from my refrigerator and handed me one. He pointed out the laundry window with his bottle. "Intruder out there."

The orange cat sat motionless in the middle of the backyard, staring at the back door. It looked like a mottled terracotta statue.

I took a bowl of milk out to the cat. It sat calmly enough

until I got within ten feet or so, then it backed off and waited for me put the bowl down. Then I backed off, and the cat padded to the bowl and began to lap at the milk. Every few seconds it looked up at me.

"Later, Cat," I said, "Too much work to do."

Going into the house, I hoped Cowboy hadn't heard me talking to Cat. Not Cat, dammit, a cat. Don't want to get carried away over the mangy thing.

Cowboy and I mulled over the problem with another beer. It seemed Carl Dresden was the key. He was our only link to the hitter. Noonebury was after Dresden, too, of course, and it was unlikely we could find him first, but still … Besides, even getting close might give us a lead. And, damn it, you don't get hits if you never swing at the ball.

It was just after five when I phoned the Mini-Maxi Food Barn office number. It rang seven times; I thought they'd closed for for the day; then a woman answered.

"Mini-Maxi, how may I help you?" She sounded out of breath.

"Hi, there, sugarplum," I said. "Lemme talk to Carl, will ya?"

"Mr. Dresden's not here, sir."

"Well, he damn well should be! We got a big problem with this order of Idaho po— tell you what, sweetie-babe, when do you expect old Carl anyway? And what'd you say your name was, dumpling?"

Across the room, Cowboy rolled his eyes.

"This is Sharon, sir. Mr. Dresden is out of town. I don't know when he'll be back." She'd caught her breath; now she sounded irritated.

"Out of town where, Sharon? I'm not kidding, we need to get this—"

"Houston, sir! He's supposed to be at a Holiday Inn in

Houston. They say he's there but he's *not* there; I can't reach him, and Mr. Krandorff has been—" She caught herself abruptly. I was wrong about her being irritated; she was frustrated and nervous. When she spoke again, her voice was cooly formal. "I'm very sorry, sir, but I cannot help you. Please try again later in the week."

"Well, okay, Sharon baby, if you say so. Hey, is old Carl still living out there on Ashgrove?" The phone book on my lap listed a Dresden, Carl, but phone books aren't as good as they used to be. Too many unlisted numbers.

"Yes, sir, that's right," she said. "Do you have the number?"

I read the Dresden listing from the book; she agreed that was it. She finally remembered to ask me who I was.

"This here's Wally, dumpling. Gotta go now. Bye."

I hung up as she was saying, "Sir, Wally wh—?"

Cowboy finished his beer and shook his head. "Why do you fart around calling secretaries sugar baby and dumpling and all that crap?"

"To distract them," I said. "They get all steamed about what a sexist bastard I am, and they don't think about all the information they're handing out. Sometimes, anyway. This woman wasn't hiding anything, though; she's just overloaded. One partner dead and the other one missing; she's probably getting hassled by cops, customers, employees, everybody."

"Real nice of you to join in," Cowboy said.

"Don't rub it in. You want to hit the street?"

Cowboy shrugged. "Sure thing. We gonna hit his office or his house?"

"Beats me. It depends on what sort of guy he is. I assume we're looking for a phone number or a note; something like that. How about we start with his house, then try his office if we have to? Maybe he kept a desk diary."

Cowboy stood up and stretched. "Let's do it."

"I'll call his house first. See if anyone's home."

"Bring your gadget," he said. "Phone from the car. If you're gonna be a yuppie, do it right."

"True. Shall we stop and buy a Cuisinart, too?"

———

Carl Dresden lived in an older neighborhood, in a thirty-year old frame house that looked comfortable but not quite uptown enough for the owner of a convenience store chain.

Not quite uptown doesn't mean Dresden's house didn't have all the suburban touches, though. It had a big lawn with a sprinkler system, and it had a picket fence and a separate garage. And it had a delivery truck parked across the street. And two men sitting in an unmarked Dodge in front of the next door neighbor's. And on the other side of the Dresden house, a "yardman" followed a lawn mower back and forth over the same strip of already mowed grass.

"Well, looky there," Cowboy said. "Everybody wants to find this Dresden dude, don't they?"

"Let's try his office."

———

It was dark when we got there. Mini-Maxi Food Barn was one of three firms in a small single-story office building in Richardson. There were company signs out front, including a miniature of the rotating barn I'd seen the night Max Krandorff died.

I lurched into the empty parking area, popping the clutch

and gas to make the Mustang hop and buck. It stalled conveniently in the middle of the lot. I got out and poked around under the hood. Cowboy stayed in the car.

The building had halfhearted lights along the front, probably to discourage burglars. The Mini-Maxi office was dark; the other firms had night-lights burning inside.

"Car in the drive-in across the street is watching this place in its mirrors," Cowboy said.

"Come on," I said. "You can't tell that from here." I wiggled a wire like I knew what the wire did.

"The passenger lit a cigarette. I saw it in both mirrors. If I can see him, he can see me. Simple."

"Very good." I'd have to remember that one. "And that's another department Dodge on the cross street, or I'll eat your hat, snakeskin band and all."

I stepped back, dusted my hands, and dropped the hood. The motor started with no more complaint than usual. We left.

"Well now, boss-man," Cowboy said, "it looks like they done put a crimp in our style."

"Not really," I said. "All we have to do is chase the cops away from Dresden's house. Then we can burgle it."

"Uh-huh. And how you gonna do that?"

"Simple, Igor," I said in the Transylvanian accent that bugs Hilda so much. "Watch this one."

21

"This high tech gizmo is going to be more help than I thought," I told Cowboy as we pulled away from a McDonald's drive-in window five minutes from Dresden's house. He held the bags of food on his lap and watch me fumble with Ed's fancy phone.

"Watch where you're going, boss-man," he muttered. He put the bags on the floor and peered out the Mustang's windshield suspiciously. I didn't know what bothered him; there wasn't all that much traffic.

I juggled the steering wheel and the phone handset and a scrap of paper with Dresden's home phone number on it, and simultaneously swerved to miss an ancient Plymouth with a death wish. Maybe there was more to this car phone business than I'd realized. Driving while phoning was harder than it looked.

Cowboy shifted in his seat and said, "How 'bout I drive if you're gonna play with that thing?"

"It's all right," I said. "Just punch in this number, will you?"

Cowboy took the handset and paper, tapped briefly, and handed back the handset.

"Will you at least stop while you're talking?"

"Keep it down," I said. "It's ringing."

Cowboy shifted in his seat again.

A woman answered Dresden's phone by repeating the number.

"Good evening," I said, "this is Lloyd Hopgood at the airport message center. Is that Mrs. Dresden?"

"Stoplight coming up," Cowboy hissed at me. He didn't have to; I'd already seen it. Really.

"Yes, this is Mrs. Dresden," the woman on the phone said. Her speech was slow and precise. Six margaritas would do that. So would old-school formality; I couldn't tell yet which was affecting her.

I said, "Message from Mr. Dresden. It says, 'Arriving …' ah, where did that go …?"

I tried to look at my watch, drive, and hold the phone all at once. Cowboy noticed, made a gargling noise, and shoved his wrist in front of my face. His watch said eight thirty-five.

"Right, Mrs. Dresden, here we are. 'Arriving nine-thirty. Meet me at message center.' Signed: Carl."

"This is most unusual, Mr. Hopgood," she said. "Carl always phones me himself." Her tone of voice said she was old-school formal, not drunk, and the tiniest bit miffed at that naughty Carl.

"Yes, ma'am. I wouldn't know about that. This message asks you to pick him up."

"Which airline is he on?"

"I don't know, Mrs. Dresden. All the airlines send messages through—"

A semitrailer thundered around the Mustang and cut back into my lane. I realized I had slowed to about twenty and mashed the gas pedal. Cowboy fidgeted with his hat and said, "Goddamn." Then he said it again.

"What on earth was that noise, Mr. Hopgood?" said Mrs. Dresden.

"Landing aircraft," I said. Maybe Cowboy was right after all. I swerved into a loading zone and stopped. The driver of a station wagon slowed and yelled several words Mrs. Dresden probably didn't know. I said into the phone, "Do you want me to repeat the message?"

"No, Mr. Hopgood. I have it. Nine-thirty at the message center. Where exactly *is* the message center?"

"Between Delta and American, ma'am. You can't miss it." I wondered if there really was anything between Delta and American. "And we're at Dallas-Fort Worth airport, ma'am, not Love Field."

The round-trip to D-FW would take her at least an hour, plus however long she searched for Lloyd Hopgood and the "message center." Plenty of time.

"The big airport," she said dutifully. "I understand. Thank you, Mr. Hopgood."

She hung up gently; I clipped the handset back into place and turned to Cowboy. "She bought it."

"Let's go see if the cops buy it, too," he said. "But slowly, Mr. Hopgood. Slo-o-o-wly."

I pulled out into traffic again. "I don't know about you, Cowboy. You must be getting old."

"I hope to," he said. "I surely do hope to do that."

———

I parked a block and a half from the Dresden house and found my old binoculars in the pile of junk on the backseat. We ate

Quarter-pounders with cheese and drank coffee and waited to see what happened when Mrs. Dresden left. If she left.

"You reckon this Noonebury dude has her phone tapped?" Cowboy said.

"Probably. I would."

"Hah! Man who'd drive and play Harvey Hopalong all at the same time would do most anything."

At eight fifty-eight a large dark car gingerly backed out of the Dresden driveway. It came our way, moving slowly in and out of the streetlights' glow. It was a four-year-old Chrysler. The woman driving it sat rigidly upright and craned her neck to see over the wheel.

I said, "Wal, dagnab it, that there is Miz Carl Dresden, as Ah live and breathe."

Cowboy groaned. "You sound 'bout as country as Dan Quayle," he said. "What're the cops doing?"

With the binoculars and good street lighting, I could see well enough to do a full play-by-play. "The lawn mower's gone," I said. "Even Noonebury's Scotsmen don't mow lawns at night. Although I suppose it would save on sunli—Here we go! Two of 'em getting out of the Dodge now. Uh-huh, and from the truck we have ... one, ah, two more. Quick huddle in the middle of the street, and bingo! Everybody into the Dodge; way to go, guys ... and they're off!"

We ducked down as the Dodge rushed past, then sat up grinning. "Would you care to join me in a small housebreaking?" I said.

"Might as well," Cowboy said. "This coffee's cold now."

22

We left the Mustang parked where it was and walked down the street toward Dresden's house. Without discussing it, we stepped off the curb together and went first to the fake delivery truck.

"Rafferty, you're almost as suspicious as me sometimes," Cowboy said.

"My cynicism is a rock," I said, "a stable guidepost in a changing, troubled world."

"Damn," Cowboy said. "Now I'm sorry I mentioned it."

The truck had a catering-company name painted in fat cartoon-style letters. Dozens of polka dots in various sizes and colors surrounded the lettering; At least three of the small black polka dots weren't painted on; they were holes in the sheet metal, with sliding or lifting covers on the inside.

Cowboy said, "Probably close 'em up so folks don't spray-paint their pretty camera lenses."

"Spray paint is good," I said. "I had only thought of smeary fingerprints or masking tape."

There were other disguised camera ports in the rear doors of the truck and on the opposite side. None of the ports were open. I tapped one of the ports and said, "Come out, come out, wherever you are."

"Got a better way than that," Cowboy whispered. He found the truck's gas cap and fumbled it off noisily. Then he talked to the side of the truck and dared me to drop a lighted match into the gas tank.

There was no reaction from inside the truck. The intrepid Scotsmen had abandoned their fancy truck, apparently without a second thought.

"This ain't even tough enough to be interesting," Cowboy said. "House'll prob'ly be unlocked and all."

"Come on," I said. "She won't be gone very long." It was nine-eleven.

The house was not unlocked, though it might as well have been. The Dresdens had thoughtfully installed a window air-conditioner in the ground floor master bedroom. Cowboy lifted the window a few more inches, I lifted out the air-conditioner, and Cowboy crawled in through the hole. We reinstalled the air-conditioner, Cowboy unlocked the back door for me, and we were both inside by nine-seventeen.

No wonder burglary is a growth industry.

We did a quick walk-through first, to get the feel of the place. There was a promising-looking desk in the master bedroom. From a framed picture on the desk, Carl Dresden and, presumably, Mrs. Dresden smiled out at the room. She was a small, birdlike woman with perfect hair and makeup. She looked exactly like she sounded.

"That Dresden?" Cowboy said.

"That's him."

"Wimpy-lookin dude, ain't he?"

The rest of the house was tidy, teetering on the brink of sterile, and not quite as large as it appeared from the outside. Upstairs we found two more bedrooms, a bath, and what appeared to be a general-purpose work-and-storage room. Large cardboard boxes were stacked neatly in one corner. They had labels like Amy's Clothes and Winter Bedding. A built-in counter ran the full length of the wall opposite the door. There was a sewing project under way on one end of the counter; a notepad and two shoe boxes on the other end.

"Might as well start here," Cowboy said.

"Go ahead. Let's say ten-twenty as bug-out time. She can't be back before then."

I left him there and went downstairs to rifle the desk in the master bedroom.

It turned out to be Mrs. Dresden's desk. She kept meticulous records of clothing purchases, household appliance warranties, and the fluctuating fortunes of a hundred shares of General Motors. Sadly she didn't keep files on hired killers. Undaunted, I pressed on.

The adjoining bathroom didn't tell me much. She dyed her hair. He shaved with a blade razor. Big deal.

In their walk-in closet, the layout was him left, her right, with a wicker laundry hamper in the middle.

Dresden had a few suits, but the most common items were slacks and plain sports shirts. His clothes were decent quality, middle of the range, neat but unimaginative, heavy on grays and blues.

Mrs. Dresden dressed a touch better; she had a few dresses I thought might be expensive, and she was a proponent of the Imelda Marcos theory of footwear acquisition. Except for her shoes, though, neither of them was a clotheshorse. Maybe that was useful information, but I couldn't see how.

I guessed which dresser was Carl's on the first try. Not much there—underwear, socks, golf sweaters, the usual. I checked the bedside tables. A floral handkerchief, sleep mask, and *The Clan of the Cave Bear* on her side, half a box of man-size Kleenex on his. I don't know what I expected; Dresden wasn't the type to have a bedroom gun. Or any gun, for that matter.

It was ten-fifteen, almost time to go. I'd struck out in the bedroom, so I used the remaining minutes to prowl the ground floor.

The Dresdens had one of those combined seat-and-tele-phone-table things in the hall near the foot of the stairs. The drawer had a pop-up index gadget inside. The entries were written in a man's hand, but many of them had been scratched through or amended with notes like "until 12/86." The gadget was dusty, and the spring was hesitant; it didn't feel like it was still in active use. I put it back in the bottom of the drawer.

There was also a booklet with a floral-design cover in the drawer. It was full of telephone numbers, too, but they were in a feminine handwriting. I put that one back, too, and checked my watch. Ten twenty-one.

I was about to whistle for Cowboy when he came down the stairs. "Find anything?" I said.

"Not so's you'd notice it. The bedrooms up there are guest rooms. Used to be kids' rooms, looks like. The only good stuff was in the shoe boxes in that den or whatever you call it. Paper. Lots of arithmetic. He'd been working out payment plans, budgets, things like that."

"Personal or company?" I said. "And let's roll, it's time to get out."

Cowboy sauntered toward the back of the house. "Well, I say company, but I can't be sure. It's just doodling, you under-stand. He used initials and rounded off a lot. So, twenty-five plus thirty-seven might mean dollars or hundreds or thousands."

"Or cartons of cornflakes."

"Yeah, that, too."

In the kitchen I opened the back door and set the spring latch to lock behind us. We stepped outside; Cowboy pulled the door closed and checked that it had locked.

Ninety seconds later, we were getting into the Mustang when Mrs. Dresden's Chrysler oozed sedately down the street. I resisted the impulse to wave to her.

The unmarked Dodge was close behind her, too close for a discreet tail. It stopped four doors short of her house, probably to give her time to put the car away and get inside.

I coaxed the Mustang into something approaching automotive life and we pulled away from the curb. As we passed the idling Dodge, four faces swiveled after us.

I resisted the urge to wave to them, too, but it was much more difficult.

Then the portable phone rang.

23

t was him.

"Where the hell were you?" he said. "I've been trying to call you for an hour."

"An emergency came up," I said. "I ran out of beer. Just walked in the door, as a matter of fact. What can I do for you?" I wheeled the Mustang around the corner one-handed and let it coast to a stop. I didn't want to screw up or miss anything. At the same time it annoyed me that I didn't feel confident about driving and telephoning at the same time.

"I told you to wait for my call," he said. He sounded peeved.

I looked out the car window into someone's dark lawn and hoped they didn't have a loud watchdog. "I'm here now, aren't I? You want this money or not?"

"Yeah, but ..."

"You're a hard guy to deal with," I said. "Hey, I don't even know what to call you. What's your name?"

A pause; then, "You can call me Dave."

"Okay, Dave, what happens now?"

"You give me my goddamned money," he said.

"Suits me. Where? When?"

A longer pause this time. When he finally spoke, there was a sly undertone. "The whole twenty grand?"

"Hang on. Not twenty. There's only fifteen thousand. That's all he gave me, Dan. You did say your name was Dan, didn't you?"

"Uh, no. It's … Dave."

"Oh, right. Dave. Got it now. Anyway—"

"You're a smart-ass, Rafferty. I don't like that."

"Hey, I'm scared, that's all. I mean, I was sound asleep, and that firebomb came in … hell, I could have been killed, burned up all alone in my bed. You can have the money, Don. Just stop trying to burn me."

I wasn't happy with my performance; I wanted to sound nervous, but it came out whiny. You suppose Gielgud and Olivier ever had days like that?

On the other hand, the hitter responded to whiny pretty well. "I almost shot you, asshole," he said. "You were out like a light; didn't even know I was there. Remember that, and don't try to fuck with me!" His voice got a trifle screechy there at the end.

"No problem. You're calling the shots, Dick. Tell me what you want me to do."

"Wait there. I'll call you right back." The phone clattered briefly, then went dead.

Cowboy said, "You don't do a bad grovel, boss-man."

"It wasn't good enough. He's suspicious. I think I was too anxious to hand over the money." I slipped the Mustang into gear and drove off again.

"How's he sound?" Cowboy said.

"Nervous. Cautious. I think he's using phone booths, in case we try to trace the call or lock the line. He's changing booths now, I'd say."

"Tell me about him," Cowboy said. "Never knowed anybody to load a Molotov cocktail with water before."

"Yeah, that's interesting, isn't it? As a warning it's reasonably inventive. Most people wouldn't know how to make one the right way, let alone modify it. And he knows a little bit about phone tricks and traps, too. He didn't learn that kind of thing playing Trivial Pursuit. But at the same time he's worried about meeting me to pick up the money. Hell, he's more than worried; he's downright flaky."

Cowboy said, "How'd that 'burn alone' routine go down?"

"Great. He picked up on it, bragged that he had looked through the window and seen me asleep. So the good news is he doesn't know about Hilda. She's in the clear, as long as I don't lead him to her."

We came to Central Expressway; I turned onto it and let the Mustang trundle along in the slow lane. "He gets angry," I said. "Sometimes it sounds like he's stirring himself up deliberately. For courage, maybe, or motivation; I can't tell exactly. Oh, and he gave me a phony name, then forgot what he'd said."

Cowboy blew out his breath in disgust. "When you add it all up, it says this dude ain't no pro."

"'Fraid not," I said. "Sorry about that."

"Shit," said Cowboy. "Goddamned amateurs can make you dead too easy."

"Good point."

He was right; amateurs are bad news. They don't know how to read a situation, so they pull the trigger at strange times for even stranger reasons. They're usually emotional, too, and that makes them unpredictable. But because of that unpredictability, they are sometimes very effective. Which is yet another problem with amateurs.

You can't ignore them; they're too dangerous for that.

The Mockingbird Lane exit came up. I took it and drove east, past the Dr Pepper plant. "Let's go home," I said. "If he calls back to set up a meet, I'll need a case or something to pretend I still have the money."

"Did he try a con about how much money Dresden gave you?" Cowboy said.

"Yep. He wanted to make sure I actually had the cash."

"Which was a good idea, you gotta admit that."

"Yes," I said.

"Goddamned amateurs."

"You're starting to repeat yourself."

We arrived at my house a little after eleven. The phone rang at eleven forty-five.

"That big art gallery place between Woodall Rogers Expressway and downtown," he said. "You know it?" His voice was tight.

"I'll find it."

"The parking lot," he said. "Twelve-thirty." He hung up abruptly.

"It's on," I told Cowboy.

"'Bout time," he said. "Let's go hang that sucker out to dry."

24

The Dallas Museum of Art sits well back from Harwood Street, on the northern side of the central business district. The building looks drab to me, but most people like it. Most people don't go there at one o'clock in the morning, though, and they don't stand around beside their cars, squinting out into the night, wondering who's out there.

Those people definitely have the right idea.

"What'n hell are you bitchin' about now?" Cowboy's voice floated up out of the Mustang's darkened backseat.

"I wasn't bitching," I said. "I was, ah, humming." I strolled around the car, then came back to lean on the same fender. I carried my scarred old vinyl attaché case so the hitter —goddamn it, who was he?—could see it. He was late. I was tired. And maybe Cowboy was right; maybe I did bitch a little.

"This turkey better show up soon," I said. "My feet hurt."

Cowboy's chuckle floated out of the car into the warm night air. "Hell, you might never see him," he said. "Situation like this, lotsa old boys would hang back in the dark, use a deer rifle to take you out, then come pull that case out of your cold, dead hands."

"I'm not too impressed with that scenario," I said.

The backseat chuckled again. "Oh, it'd turn all right. I'd whack him for you, don't worry about that."

"Wow, that's a relief."

Cowboy had a good point. If the hitter *was* out there with a long gun, I couldn't do much about it.

And me with all that weaponry, too. I had my big military Colt in the back of my belt, a Spanish .25 in an ankle holster, and a sawed-off shotgun crammed into the attaché case. I'd had to cut that old twelve-gauge double-barrel way, way down to get it into the case. It was too short now. Having had a chance to think about it, I didn't really want to be holding on to that thing when it went *boom*.

Way to go, Rafferty. Three guns, and not one of them much good over, say, forty yards. Maybe I could throw the shotgun at—

"Thing I can't figure," Cowboy said, "is why Dresden hired an amateur like this dude to waste his partner."

"Dresden's an amateur himself. What does he know about hiring hard men?"

"I s'pose. He paid way over the going rate, too."

"True," I said.

"And you gave all that money away," Cowboy said wistfully. "To the *cops*."

"Heads up," I said. "Company coming."

A lone car—medium-size GM; dark, maybe green—cruised up Harwood. It cautiously eased toward the curb and stopped. A man got out. He left the engine running and headlights on, and started into the parking lot, walking directly toward me.

"Come to Papa," I said softly, and reached back to grasp the comforting weight of the .45.

Cowboy didn't say anything, but there was a dry metallic click, and the Mustang shifted a fraction on its springs.

The man was still thirty yards away; still coming. The headlights of his car threw a bright corona around his shape, turned him into a two-dimensional cutout with hard edges, but no detail. Both his hands were free, though. And empty. Why?

I stepped away from the Mustang, holding the attaché case in front of me. The man stopped abruptly.

"Hey, somebody there?" He leaned forward from the waist and wobbled as he peered into the dark. "Whozat anyway?"

I moved around in an arc to get his car's lights out of my eyes. His head didn't follow me; he kept peering at where I'd been.

"Shit-fire, anybody there or not?" he said.

He sounded so obviously drunk, I was sure it was a gimmick. I looked around to make sure no one was coming up behind me, then pointed the Colt at him and said, "How're you doing for Molotov cocktails tonight?"

"Oops! Knew there was somebody there. Pearl for me buddy, but"—he fumbled with his zipper—"the damn stuff goes right through me. Drink a can and piss a quart, swear to God."

His belch blended with the splash of water as he urinated on the asphalt.

After a long time—he was almost right about that quart— he sighed happily, zipped up, turned unsteadily, and stomped back toward his car.

"Drop in anytime," I said.

Back in his car he screeched his starter motor trying to

start the idling engine, then lurched away with a sharp tire chirp. I walked back to the Mustang.

"Forget it," I said. "False alarm."

"What the hell was all that about?" Cowboy said.

I told him. The car shook for several seconds.

It was well past one o'clock. Every four or five minutes a car scuttled past on the lighted street. Mostly, though, nothing happened.

"You know," I said, "Dresden's wife didn't seem very upset. A little, maybe, but not much. You'd think she'd be climbing the walls, what with hubby gone and the cops pestering her."

"Maybe they haven't talked to her yet," Cowboy said. "Maybe they don't want to spook her, figure to wait and see which way she jumps."

"Maybe."

At one-thirty I said, "This jerk is not coming. No way. He's giving me time to give up and go home; then he's going to call with another location."

Cowboy grunted. "Maybe, maybe not. You and me, we was in his shoes, we wouldn't be in no hurry. We'd hide somewheres and just watch for an hour or two. 'Specially if we didn't trust the opposition to play fair."

"We're pros," I said. "He's an amateur."

"Yeah, but, for an amateur, this dude's got some pretty good moves."

"True, damn it," I said.

At one forty-five, we decided to wait until two o'clock. A few minutes before two, though, a DPD prowl car went by twice, cruising slowly, being oh-so-cool.

Why explain messy details like sawed-off shotguns? We left while the prowl car was on the other side of the block.

Cowboy complained about "goddamned amateurs" all the way to my house.

I was wrong about the hitter; he didn't phone again. So now he was a wild card. He might do anything, or nothing. Cowboy was right. Goddamned amateurs.

We split what little remained of the night into two-hour segments and took turns sleeping and watching.

During my first watch I put a bowl of milk out back for the visiting cat, but it never showed up.

I came on duty again at six-thirty on Tuesday morning, eye-gritty and brain-fogged, far too groggy to enjoy the cool dawn. The milk bowl was empty.

Cowboy said the cat had dropped by while I slept. "It ain't such a bad-looking critter," he said, "if you happen to like cats."

Then he went back to bed and left me to blink and scratch and work out what we were going to do next.

25

Noon Tuesday. My house. The hitter still had not phoned. "Hell with this," I said to Cowboy. "Let's go back to Plan A."

He looked up from his plate of ham and eggs. "I forget what Plan A is, exactly."

"That is the one where we don't wait around for this stupid phone to ring. We backtrack through Dresden to find the hitter."

Cowboy nodded and pushed his hat half an inch higher on his forehead. I wondered if he wore his hat at the breakfast table at home. Probably. Mimi probably wore hers, too.

"Oh, that Plan A," Cowboy said. "The one where we break into Dresden's house, wander around with our thumbs in our ears, then leave with nothing to show for it."

"Go to hell. Today we'll do better. I have an idea."

Cowboy nodded again. "Well, as long as you've got an idea ..."

We walked up Carl Dresden's sidewalk at two-thirty, after running Noonebury's surveillance gauntlet. The fake catering truck was gone today. There was another department Dodge at the curb, though, and across the street a workman in a Dallas Power & Light uniform didn't seem to know what he was looking for in the bottom of a utilities access hole.

"Do they seem awfully obvious to you?" I said, as we stepped up onto the front porch.

Cowboy sniffed. "Funny thing for you to say, walking around in a suit like that."

There was nothing wrong with my suit. It was light gray mostly, with a very small black jiggly pattern that made the suit seem dark gray from more than a foot away. I thought it was pretty classy.

"Suit looks like it's made out of that screen door stuff," Cowboy said.

I pushed the doorbell button. "Never mind the suit," I said. "The real problem is this dumb tie. Twice in one week is a bad precedent. And I haven't figured out how to explain you."

Cowboy had flatly refused to wear anything remotely resembling a working cop's wardrobe. He had his usual boots, jeans, western shirt and hat. So there.

"You'll think of something," he said. "Tell her I'm a Texas Ranger."

Then there were rapid footsteps inside the house, and the front door opened. Mrs. Dresden swiveled her head from me to Cowboy and back again. The action was like her picture come to life—darting and birdlike.

"Mrs. Carl Dresden?" I said formally.

"Yesss. What is it?" More head-darting, but apparently only honest confusion in her bright blue eyes.

I flapped my wallet at her, to give her a quarter-second

glimpse of my honorary deputy sheriff's card and a dime-store plastic badge. "Detective Inspector Ptarmigan," I said. "This is Sergeant Eider. We'd like to ask you a few questions."

Cowboy shuffled and grunted beside me, then slowly took off his hat and drawled, "Howdy, ma'am." Only a professional Texan could take a corny line like that and turn it into a courtly romanticism. He did. She loved it. She preened and twittered.

I decided not to bother with my story that Cowboy was an undercover cop on the stockyard detail.

"Oh, my," Mrs. Dresden said, "this must be about poor Maxwell. Do come in, officers, please."

Cowboy smirked at me as we filed past her. Inside, she wondered aloud about where we should sit for our chat. She offered, and we declined, coffee, tea, lemonade, and whatever was next on the list.

We went into the living room. Mrs. Dresden fluttered across the room to fiddle with the fold on a drape, then came back to plump a cushion. She was one of those people who seem to be in constant motion but never accomplish anything noticeable.

She finally maneuvered Cowboy and me into overstuffed chairs, and she landed on a floral-patterned couch. Even then she kept reaching out to adjust magazines on the coffee table, pluck imagined fluff off her couch, and rearrange her skirt around her legs. It made me tired just to watch her work that hard.

"We're investigating the, uh, death of Mr. Max Krandorff."

Mrs. Dresden nodded. "Yes, I thought that might be it."

"I hate to trouble you with this, Mrs. Dresden. I'd rather talk to your husband, but he seems to be out of town." I took out my notebook and flipped through it. A few seconds of frowns and notebook-flipping always puts the final polish on the fake-cop routine. With me, you get all the optional extras.

"Oh, yes," she said. "Carl's in Houston on business." She took a dainty handkerchief out of her left sleeve, fiddled with it then put it back.

"Yes, ma'am," I said. "That's what I was told at his office. A person named, uh ..." I frowned at the notebook page with a new barbecue sauce recipe and said, "Can't quite read my own—"

"Sharon, perhaps. Sharon Palmerston?" She turned to Cowboy and said confidentially, "Sharon practically runs that office. I don't know how they'd get along without her."

"That's it," I said. "Palmerston." I wrote it down. The woman I'd talked to yesterday was named Sharon. "Mrs. Dresden, where is your husband staying in Houston?"

She smiled. "At the Holiday Inn. Carl always stays at Holiday Inns."

I said, "When did he leave for Houston, ma'am?" I'm not proud; if down-home stuff like "ma'am" works, I go with it.

She frowned prettily and touched a fingertip to her lips. "Why, um, last Wednesday. I remember because it was the very night when Number Three was held up and Max was ... well, you know."

"Yes. Have you spoken to your husband since then, Mrs. Dresden?"

"Of course! Carl was beside himself with grief. They were close, you know. Some business partners aren't, I know, but Carl and Max, well ..."

We tsk-tsked over the injustice of it all; then I said, "Did you phone your husband, or did he phone you?"

"Now let me think ... I believe he phoned me, because— Yes, he did! I had just hung up from speaking to Sharon. She called me—a darling girl, Sharon—so I wouldn't hear about poor Maxwell on the news first, you know, and right after that the phone rang, and it was Carl." She leaned forward, suddenly anxious. "Is that important?"

I smiled at her. "Just a routine question, ma'am. Have you phoned him in Houston since then?"

"Oh, certainly. Twice—no, I tell a lie—three times. The last time was only last night. Late. After a totally incompetent airline employee said Carl was coming home and needed a ride. You wouldn't believe it; I spent *hours* at the airport waiting and Carl never—"

"Pardon me, Mrs. Dresden. You say you phoned him last night?" This sounded like pay dirt.

"Yes, that's right, officer." She smiled at me encouragingly, I suddenly remembered a schoolteacher somewhere who had looked at me like that on the rare occasions when I got lucky with algebra.

"And where did you phone him, Mrs. Dresden?"

"Why, at the Holiday Inn, Inspector. Where else would I leave a message for him?"

Cowboy nodded to himself and seemed to melt farther into his chair.

I said to Mrs. Dresden, "Bear with me, please. I want to make sure I understand this. You called him last night?"

"Yes." Smiling more encouragement.

"At the Holiday Inn."

"Yes."

"But you didn't talk to him, because he wasn't in his room. So you left a message, and he called you back."

"Well, Carl hasn't called me back *yet*," she said, "but he will. He's very busy, you understand. The poor dear works far too hard."

"The other times you phoned him, how long did it take him to call you back?"

"Oh, I have no idea. A few hours, perhaps."

"But always the same day?" I said. "Not the next day?"

"Well, one time it was the next day, I think. Why on earth are you asking me all these things? Just phone Carl; he'll tell you whatever you want to know."

"Yes, ma'am, we'll do that," I said.

26

Mrs. Dresden smiled at me from her perch on the couch, while I pretended to read a blank page in my notebook and wondered how to play it from here.

Kevin Noonebury would have a long wait until this woman did anything incriminating. She was clean. I'd have bet money on that. When people lie to you often enough, you learn to recognize it.

"Mrs. Dresden," I said, "I'm sorry to say we're not making much progress in finding the people who killed Mr. Krandorff."

"Oh, my," she said. She held her head tilted slightly to the right, and she paid very close attention to what I said. Which didn't make it any easier.

"I'd like to have a look at … uh, does your husband have an office here at home?" Nearly messed up there, Rafferty.

"Carl uses a corner of my sewing room sometimes for his business work." She smiled. "Though he likes to say that I use three corners of his office."

I said, "We'd like to have a look at the room, please."

I avoided the word *search*, because that puts people off. Trouble was, the only euphemism I could think of was "have a look at." Weak, Rafferty. Very weak, actually, because I was thinking in terms like loot and plunder.

"Oh, my," she said again. "How very strange. Why would you want to do a thing like that?" She frowned and reminded me of that algebra teacher again. This time I wasn't doing so well.

"There may be some reference to, uh, Mr. Krandorff. Clues to who—"

"But that was a robber who killed poor Maxwell. Wasn't it? That's what Carl said."

"Yes, ma'am, it probably was. But we have to look at ever poss—"

Cowboy interrupted me with a soft drawl so loaded with Texas gallantry, it dribbled on its way to Mrs. Dresden. "We'd surely 'preciate your help here." He pronounced it *hep hair*. "Surely we would, ma'am."

Cowboy smiled at her, too, a down-home, aw-shucks, country-boy smile that melted Mrs. Dresden like an ice cream cone on a noon sidewalk.

"Well, if it's important," she said, getting up. "I'll show you where it is." Cowboy untolded himself from the soft chair and towered over the small woman. She looked up at him and said, "I'll have coffee and cake ready when you're done."

I said, "Don, why don't you help Mrs. Dresden with the coffee. It won't take me a minute to, ah, examine the room for clues."

Mrs. Dresden turned toward me. "What a wonderful idea. It's right up the stairs, Inspector. On your left."

Behind and above her, Cowboy glared at me. He mouthed

"Don? *Don Eider*?" and grimaced. But he had that slow, sleepy grin back in place when Mrs. Dresden beamed back at him and said, "Come with me, Sergeant. I do hope you like chocolate cake. I put nuts in it, you see, because Carl …"

They disappeared into the kitchen. I went up the stairs like a rat up a drainpipe. The two shoe boxes we'd seen before were still on the counter in the workroom, sewing room, office, what ever the hell it was.

The boxes were loaded with paper, apparently stuffed in at random. There were a couple of wire-bound steno pads, pages torn from several different scratch pads, and folded sheets of typing paper. Some of the scribbles were do-this, do-that reminders, but most of what I saw in a quick riffle was financial calculations. As Cowboy had said, it was too abbreviated and unlabeled to decode here.

I tucked both boxes under my arm and carried them downstairs. At the bottom of the stairs, I took Dresden's telephone number gadget out of the phone-table drawer and put it into the boxes. I prowled around a little more, too, but didn't find anything particularly interesting.

There was a screened porch on the back of the house; I slipped out that way to get the loot past Mrs. Dresden in the kitchen and the Noonebury surveillance teams out front. I carried the boxes through the backyard and left them under a bush by the gate from the alley.

On the way back to the house, I noticed a door in the back wall of the separate garage. It was unlocked. Never could pass up an unlocked door.

Inside, the garage was typical. Messier than most, maybe, but still tidier than mine. Mrs. Dresden's Chrysler was there. The other parking bay was empty. Whatever Carl drove, it was probably parked in an airport lot somewhere. That was a shame. It would have been useful to toss Dresden's car.

The Chrysler hadn't been out for several hours; its hood was cool. I don't know why I checked that. Some things you do by reflex action, I guess.

I was leaving the garage, going out through the back door again, when I noticed a pile of magazines in a big garbage can half filled with papers and bottles. The magazines were the top layer of trash, the latest things to be thrown out. I picked them out of the garbage and spread them across the hood of Mrs. Dresden's Chrysler.

They were all gun, survivalist, or quasi-military magazines like the one he'd carried the day he approached me downtown. One of them might have been the same magazine; I couldn't remember well enough. Some were current issues, newsstand pristine and apparently unthumbed. Others were far out of date, soiled and dog-eared. There were some I recognized and some I didn't. They had titles like *Firefight*, *Aftermath*, and *Combat Action*. I found myself grinning broadly. I had a good feeling about those magazines.

I scooped them into a pile, carried them outside, and hid them with the shoe boxes of papers.

Then I sneaked back into the house and let Mrs. Dresden hear me clump around.

"Oh, there you are, Inspector!" she said, and smiled as she wagged a finger at me. "Hurry now. Poor Sergeant Eider is waiting for his cake."

We sat at the dining room table, used the good china, and looked at two thousand snapshots of the Dresden grandchildren who lived in a place named—I swear this is true—Succasunna, New Jersey.

I couldn't tell Billy from Donny, or remember which of them played Little League ball, and I didn't even have a second helping of cake. That pile of goodies outside gnawed at me. All those juicy clues waiting to lead me to the hitter. I was on to him. I could feel it.

Rafferty's Rule Twenty: Any hunch so strong it hurts just has to be right.

I hoped.

27

"Now I understand how he's doing it," I said to Hilda. "It's pretty cute. Dresden flew to Houston —probably flew, anyway, too much driving otherwise—and checked into a hotel."

We were sitting on Hilda's living room floor, surrounded by my booty from Dresden's house. I waved a survivalist magazine as a pointer and expounded Rafferty's Theory of Dresdenivity.

"After he checked in, the sneaky bastard boogied away into the dark, dark night. So, officially, he's there. He's not hiding, oh, no. The hotel registration records prove it. But he's not there, not really. What he's doing, babe, is phoning in every once in a while to get any messages. Betcha. He might be actually going back to the hotel, but I doubt that. Using the phone is safer."

Hilda put her coffee mug on a coaster in the midst of the debris. "Why would he use such a complicated routine?"

"To keep his options open. Eventually, if the dust settles, Dresden can surface with a song and dance like *'Boy, have I been busy! Work, work, work. And by the way, did anything inter-esting happen while I was gone?"'*

Hilda said, "Won't the hotel wonder about him being away from his room all the time? They'd worry about getting paid wouldn't they?"

"No problem. Once the old credit card's been through the imprinter, the hotel doesn't care if he sleeps in the room, or uses it to store his suitcase, or just likes to walk around with the key in his pocket. Hell, he's not breaking any laws down there."

"Hmm." Hilda said.

"Couldn't have put it better myself," I said. I tossed the magazine onto the pile of others like it and drank some beer. Thirsty work, expounding theories. "Now, here comes the really cute part, Hil. If the dust *doesn't* settle, if the cops start looking seriously for Dresden, he has a big head start. Hell, they'd still be talking to the Holiday Inn desk clerk while Dresden cinched up his seat belt and placed his seat back in the upright position. Next stop: Rio."

Hilda looked at her watch. So did I. Seven-fifty; well past hungry. Cowboy and Mimi had gone for Mexican food and would be back any minute. None too soon, either.

Hilda said, "Who, exactly, is this man Dresden hiding from? The police, the man he hired to kill his partner, or you? Or all three of you?"

"You mean all two of us. Remember, Dresden thinks I'm the one he hired to kill Max."

"Maybe not," she said. "He thought that when he gave you the money, but he may know better by now. After all, the real killer apparently has some way to contact him. And if he does know that he paid the wrong person, he'd hide from both of you, right?"

"That's good, Hil. And it might explain why the hitter runs so hot and cold about contacting me."

"Because he's looking for Dresden, too," she said. "Trying to get his fee from either one of you, and he doesn't care which."

"Right," I said. "You're very good at this, babe. I'm surrounded by talented amateurs this time."

Hilda stood up and ruffled my hair. "Running you ragged are they, big guy?"

"Cowboy and I are chugging along. We're getting there." I got up, too, and we started to set the dining table.

"Chugging is the right word," Hilda said. "I'm sorry about that car."

I shrugged. "It got us here."

It was an ancient Rambler from an el cheapo car rental company I had never heard of. This afternoon, after we'd picked up the things I'd swiped from Dresden's house, I had decided to fall back and regroup at Hilda's. While I changed from my suit to comfortable clothes, Cowboy arranged for Mimi to drop a car at the parking garage we'd selected for a cutout point.

We left my house with no sign of the hitter or his white Tempo, doubled back more often than we needed to, and finally drove to the big garage and searched for whatever car Mimi had rented for us.

"You should have seen us," I told Hilda. "I swear that place had forty floors. And we must have checked every car on every floor, looking for the one with a green ribbon on the rearview mirror and a copy of *Western Horseman* on the back shelf."

Hilda stood in one spot, leaned over the table, and distributed four place mats and plates. I walked around and around the table, dealing out silverware. Memo to behavioral science department: there's a doctoral thesis on gender differences in table setting just waiting to be snapped up.

"Finally," I said, "way the hell up in a corner on the top floor, we found the Rambler Mimi rented. There was a pickup parked next to it, a pickup with one of those little campers on the back. Not the walk-in kind, just a low roof over the bed. Ah, I say *bed* deliberately here, because there was a bed in there, and a couple who were, shall we say, locked in the throes of passion."

Hilda said, "Don't come a-knockin' when this van's a rockin'."

"You got it. Plus, there were two other guys standing around, leaning on cars. Hanging out, being cool. Soon as they saw us, one of them came down with a sudden case of 'Feet, don't fail me now.'"

Hilda put a napkin beside each plate. She put two extra napkins at my place. I don't know why it is, but I always seem to get the drippy tacos.

"Cowboy and I figured it for a gang rape. We bailed out of the Mustang. I grabbed the guy who'd tried to rabbit, and Cowboy damn near ripped the back flap off that camper top. But the woman inside just smiled and called him honey and told him to wait his turn."

"Oh, really," Hilda said.

"Yeah. It turned out she's a hooker. That was her camper. I don't know how she operates exactly. Maybe she drives around till she gets a full truckload, then parks to work off the backlog. Whatever."

Hilda shook her head slowly and went to the kitchen for glasses. When she came back, I put the glasses around the table and said, "Well, you know how much weaponry Cowboy lugs around; he feels naked unless he's fully outfitted for World War III. We had to shift Cowboy's armory from the Mustang to the Rambler. We didn't need an audience for that, so we chased the two guys away. Pretty soon the third guy, the one who was in the camper, came out. Maybe he finished; maybe Cowboy put him off his stroke, I don't know. Anyway, we ran him off, too."

Hilda put a vase of flowers in the center of the table. We went into the kitchen. She got out serving dishes and platters and put them on the counter.

"But," I said, "funny part was when the hooker came out. First, though, she saw me and offered her services. Free, naturally. Probably wanted something to remember during her twilight years—"

"Naturally," Hilda said.

"—but then she realized we'd scared away her customers. I never saw a woman get so mad so fast. She accused us of restraint of trade and harassment and violating her civil rights."

"That's it!" Hilda put her fists on her hips. "Rafferty, if you think I'm going to believe this one, you're crazy," she said. "You got me last week with that flasher-in-a-wheelchair story. I admit that, but not this one. No way!"

"Hil, baby, would I lie about—?"

"Yes," Hilda said. "You would."

"Anyway, the hooker carried on until Cowboy said he'd let the air out of her tires. She called that 'preempting her economic potential.' I assume that meant she couldn't cruise for customers on four flat tires. So she left and—"

Cowboy and Mimi arrived then. The kitchen became crowded with people and food wrappers and spicy aromas. There may well be things that smell better than Mexican food, but I'd have argued about it at the time.

While we put burritos and tacos and frijoles and chili Colorado into serving dishes, Hilda said to Mimi, "Wait until you hear Rafferty's latest tall tale. He claims they met a prosti-tute who talks like an economist. It's hilarious, the stories he makes up."

Cowboy frowned at me. "Economist? Said she was a law student, didn't she? Thought she said law student anyway."

"I rest my case," I said.

Hilda and Mimi looked at each other. "It could be," Mimi said. "With these two, you just never know."

We ate then. Cowboy had also brought Mexican beer to go with the food. An inspired move. I got stuck with the drippy tacos again—what else?—but it was a great meal.

At least it was great until halfway through my third taco, when my fancy portable phone began to ring in the living room. Hilda put down her fork and looked grim. Mimi attacked another burrito.

"Here we go again," Cowboy said.

I went into the living room, snagged the phone off the coffee table, and answered it.

It was him.

28

"Funny thing happened to me last night," I said. "I stood around the Museum of Art for a couple of hours, waiting for a guy who never showed up."

"Don't be a smart-ass, Rafferty," the hitter said. "Just do what you're told, unless you want to be a fucking french fry." He sounded bone-weary. His voice was flatter than before, and the threat was reflex action, a meaningless social nicety. *How you doing today? Hot enough for you? Want to be a french fry?*

I said, "Well, you see, it's just that I don't know what you want from me. You call and want the money; I say, take the money; all of a sudden you don't want the money anymore. I don't understand what's happening, and, uh, I'd like to get this wrapped up, you know?"

Gawd, did I really say that? I hate it when people say "you know."

I felt like I was several different people. I was me, standing in Hilda's living room, burping taco fumes over a high tech phone to a hired killer who thought I was hiding under a bed at my house. And I had to stay in character as that submissive wimp until I'd drawn the killer out into the open, whereupon I would be tempted to cheerfully beat the living shit out of him. Probably, though, the best thing to do was turn him over to the cops. As long as it was the right cop. Ed Durkee, say. Definitely not Kevin Noonebury.

To accomplish all that—or even *any* of that—I had promised to hand over a pile of money I didn't have to a man whose name and location I didn't know. I was getting clandestine help from one side of an interdepartmental police squabble and carefully skirting around the other side.

It was a crazy-quilt mind-set; a schizophrenic smorgasbord. When it eventually ended, I'd probably be lonely. What if I wasn't there when I needed me?

"Hell, yes, I want the money," the hitter's voice said in my ear. "How many times do I have to tell you that?" He perked up a little but only a little. Still didn't seem to have his heart in it.

I said, "And I want you to have the money. So come get it. Let's get this over with."

He made a noise that sounded half growl, half sigh. "There's a lot going on you don't—I'll get back to you."

"Hey, wait a minute!"

"You're doing good," he said, very weary now. "Keep hangin' in there by the phone; you'll be all right." He hung up.

I spat short, sharp words at the dead phone, then realized Hilda was standing in the living room doorway. Her face was still and stony. Her lips were clamped down into a thin hard line.

"Nothing new, babe. I can't seem to flush him out."

She nodded, turned, and walked away. I fumbled the phone handset back onto its bulky base and followed her. By the time I sat down at the table, she was smiling and passing chili Colorado to Mimi.

"We working tonight?" Cowboy said.

"No. He's stalling. I don't know what's going on."

Cowboy shrugged.

"I'm screwing this up somehow," I said. "I can't move him off high center."

"It ain't you," Cowboy said, "it's him. Amateurs ain't never nothing but trouble."

"Words to live by," I said.

———

Hilda woke up in the night with a convulsive jerk and a sharp intake of breath. Then she slumped and lay still, breathing heavily.

I reached for her; she rolled into my arms. "Firebomb dream?" I said.

She nodded; her chin bumped on my shoulder. She trembled. "Scary," she said. "Hold me for a minute." She wriggled tighter against me.

I could feel her heart banging away. She shivered again. I patted her back and murmured there-there noises. I felt useless and guilty. "Hil, I'm sorry. I didn't figure anything like that would happen. I took you right into the middle of it."

"It's not your fault," she said. Her heartbeat was just beginning to slow down.

"I attract that kind of trouble," I said. "By being around me, you—"

She dug her nails into my side. "Stop that. Being without you would be worse. I'd lose more than a few hours of sleep. Besides, they're getting easier to handle. Last night's dream was ... well, it was worse."

"Do you want to see anybody about it? A counselor, a shrink, anybody like that?"

"No." Hilda's voice was firm. Her heart rate was noticeably slower now. "I'm not ready to join the couch brigade, thank you."

"It's okay, babe. Lots of people have therapy."

She eased away and rolled onto her back beside me. We held hands. "I know there's no stigma attached to psychoanalysis," she said, "but I don't need a hired confidant to tell me what my problem is. I know the problem. I had a frightening experience. It's over now. There is nothing I can do about it except worry, which would be irrational and harmful. So I don't worry."

"Maybe it's me. If I—"

"Shut up. That is not an acceptable alternative. Believe me, I'm okay. I don't walk around all day in abject terror; you know that. I guess it sneaks up on me at night, that's all."

"Two nights, two nightmares. You're batting a thousand."

"Yes, but I think tonight was only because of that phone call. And honestly, it wasn't as bad. I woke up sooner, and I calmed down much faster."

I thought of her last night, ripped out of her sleep by her nightmare, waking alone and frightened. I squeezed her hand; she squeezed back. "I feel lousy, Hil. What can I do for you?"

"You love me, and you make me laugh, and I feel good when I'm with you. What else could there be?"

"Do you want to talk about it?"

Hilda said, "We are talking about it, aren't we?"

"Yeah, sure, but I meant about the nightmare itself. Only if you want to, though."

After a moment she said, "I really don't know whether talking would erase it or plant it more firmly in my mind."

"I could affect a disinterested manner and say things like 'And how did that make you feel?'"

Hilda laughed briefly. It didn't sound like she had to force it much. Some, maybe, but not much.

I said, "I could go with 'Und how did dot make you veel?' if you prefer a more traditional approach."

"Actually," she said, "I thought I might talk to a cabdriver. That way I'd be dealing with a professional, but it wouldn't cost me ninety dollars an hour."

"You'd be better off with a bartender," I said. "Great ambience."

"No," she said, "A cabdriver. That way you know where you stand, because the meter's right out there where you can see it."

After that we invented work-o-meters and installed them on people like airline pilots and typists and whoever puts the pimentos in olives. As we babbled on, I could feel Hilda relax.

After we'd run out of work-o-meter candidates, she said muzzily, "Willoo beer morra?"

"I'll be here in the morning," I said. "Then Cowboy and I are leaving again. Gotta go catch the guy on the phone."

No response; she was asleep. Her breathing had changed and slowed. Soon she began to make the softest of bubbling sounds.

"I still don't know who he is," I whispered to the darkness, "but I know how to find the son of a bitch."

29

"Here ya go," Cowboy said. "Listen to this one. 'Ex-platoon leader Vietnam wants high-risk, high-pay job.' It's got a Shreveport address. You want it on the list or not?"

"I guess so. Shreveport is only three or four hours away. For the kind of money Dresden offered, four hours of travel time is nothing."

Cowboy looked over the edge of the magazine he held. "By car, yeah, that's about right," he said. "Thing of it is, though, if we're talking about airlines, then San Francisco is only three or four hours away. Chicago, too. New York, maybe. Whole bunch of places, come to that."

"Put 'em all down, then," I said. "Damn it."

"Whoops, here's one from Australia. Some town called Wagga Wagga, of all things. I don't expect you want that one though."

"This is your captain speaking," I said. "No Australian ads. Also no Peruvian, Fijian, English, or Sri Lankan ads. No foreign ads at all."

Cowboy grinned at me. "Canada?"

"Where the hell are you finding these things? I've only got two so far."

"Well, I don't actually have a Canadian one yet. I'm just asking, in case I should run across one."

"Canada, yes. Also Mexico. Aside from that, American ads only."

"Ain't no need for you to get all bitter and twisted," Cowboy said. "This secret agent crap is your line of work, not mine."

It was nine-thirty the next morning; Cowboy and I sat in my living room, with magazines all around our feet on the coffee table. We'd left Hilda's house after she went to work. Mimi went with her. That was my idea. If Hilda felt safe during the day, maybe she'd sleep better at night. Thinking about her nightmares made me feel bad all over again.

"Not that you ain't good at this secret-agent crap," Cowboy said, picking up another magazine.

The "secret-agent crap" that annoyed Cowboy came from my belated realization that Dresden must have found the hitter through the classified sections of the magazines I'd found in his garage.

"This here's a damn good idea, if the truth be known," Cowboy said. "It fits with this dude being so squirrelly."

I went to the kitchen for more coffee and to see if the cat had shown up for its bowl of milk on the back step. It hadn't. I hoped it hadn't run away or been hit by a car.

Back in the living room, as I put the coffee mugs down, Cowboy said, "Hey now, here's another one. This old boy says he's been everything from a Green Beret to military intelligence. Wants work as a bounty hunter, mercenary, bodyguard, undercover agent, or private investigator. Got him a phone number listed here, then 'weekends only.'"

"Some wannabee who sweeps out the local hardware store

during the week," I said. "Doesn't like the idea of his wife taking messages from all those South American generals."

"Hell," Cowboy said. He pronounced it *hay-ell*. "All these guys is amateurs. Ain't no pro gonna buy an ad in here, like they was selling a used Chevy."

It was discouraging work, sifting through Dresden's magazines. I knew we wouldn't find a classified ad saying, "Hired Killer. Grocery Stores My Speciality. Phone ..." but I had hoped there would be only two or three likely ads. Instead we found twice that many in the first two magazines. It was going to be a long day.

Although there were no specific hired-killer ads, the magazines had almost everything else for sale. You could buy almost anything that would shoot, for example, from tiny .25-caliber automatics to assault rifles and combat shotguns. And there were lockpicks and compasses and dehydrated food and books with titles like *Private Investigation Made Easy* and *How to Build a Bomb with Only Three Toothpicks and a Jar of Mayonnaise*. Well, okay, I'm exaggerating about the book titles. But only a little bit.

There were dozens of ads for military-style packs, belts, and camouflage clothing. The buzzword was *cammies*. I had forgotten there were so many versions of it.

Knives were popular, too. Articles compared knives and knife-fighting techniques; ads offered every edged weapon I could think of except, perhaps, a broadsword. The trend was mostly toward what I'd always called hunting knives. Apparently they had become "survival" knives when I wasn't looking. One ad, though, bucked the trend. It touted old-fashioned switchblades, like you used to see in 1950s juvenile-delinquent movies. The ad called the switchblades "Genuine European Stilettos."

And there was a gadget that converted a pair of .22 rifles

into a hand-cranked machine gun—a Gatling gun, actually, complete with tripod and magazine boxes. "Up to 500 rounds a minute," the ad claimed. I showed it to Cowboy. "But the shoulder holster costs three thousand dollars," I said.

"Humph," he grunted. "Some of these old boys sure do like play soldier, don't they?"

That was a pretty good overview; the magazines would appeal to guys who liked to play soldier. The magazines varied. Some were mostly trash; blatant, pandering articles and poorly composed ads for obvious rip-offs.

But some weren't bad at all, especially the specialized articles and features. Some of the topics would have whipped a pacifist to a blind fury, but they were solid red meat for detail-hungry military-trivia buffs and gun enthusiasts. There was a field report on the new Galil, for example, that Israeli adaptation of the Kalashnikov assault rifle. And a think piece about the handguns preferred by various SWAT teams. And a short item … Well, anyway, it took longer to get through those magazines than I'd expected.

Even so, by one-thirty we'd been through the whole stack, cover to cover. Over sandwiches and beer, we boiled it down.

"Okay," I said. "We have seventeen possible ads, any one of which might have been placed by Dresden's hired hitter. None of the seventeen seem any more likely than any other. You agree with that?"

Cowboy swallowed a mouthful of ham and cheese and grunted. "Goddamned amateurs, every one of 'em."

"So what? Point two, and a possible problem. Most of the ads came from the oldest magazines. In fact, the current issues don't have any personal ads like that at all."

"They musta changed the law or something," Cowboy said.

"Maybe. But the ads are, what, four or five years out of

date? Some are even older. It is not going to be easy to find these people."

Cowboy shook his head. "That don't matter. You and me, we're a whole bunch better at finding folks than this Dresden fella. Ain't nothing surer than that. So, if we can't find 'em then he couldn't have found 'em, either."

"Oh, hell, yes! Of course. *That's* why Dresden had so many of these magazines," I said. "When he didn't find what he wanted in the current issues, he went to one of those used-book-and-magazine places and bought the back issues, hoping to find at least one ad that was still good."

"Thought you'd have seen that right off," Cowboy said. He gave me a deadpan look.

"Still, even though we're superheroes, this could be a long and dirty job. At least half of these ads only have cities and post office box numbers listed. Or phone numbers. And look at the names these guys use: Dagger. Striker. Archer."

"You see the one with Occupant? That guy used to be a company clerk, I bet."

"Whatever he was, he's sure as hell not listed in the phone book under the *Os*. Hell, Cowboy, there's only one of these ads with a full name given, and that's probably not legitimate."

"If it is," Cowboy said, "he's too honest or too dumb to be the dude we want." He took a big bite of sandwich and chewed contentedly.

"You got that right. I guess we can con the information out of post offices and phone companies, but ..."

Cowboy said, "Get your cop buddy to help," or something close to that. Coming from around the sandwich, it was hard to tell.

"If I have to. Another thing. These ads cover a lot of terri-tory." Cowboy, still chewing methodically, began to shake his head. "But that isn't as important as I first thought it was"—Cowboy changed to nodding—"because any of those people might have moved. Closer or farther doesn't count. What counts is whether they left forwarding addresses."

Cowboy swallowed and said, "Damn right."

"So, forget that point," I said. "It'll solve itself. The next thing is to not go off half-cocked. We might already have a line on this guy and not know it. The fact that he *might* have moved doesn't mean he really did. Maybe one of the phone numbers from an ad is also in Dresden's telephone index gadget. And we can check the addresses—well, the three Texas addresses anyway—against that list of Ford Tempo registrations."

Cowboy looked like his stomach hurt. "*More* secret-agent crap? What ever happened to the good old days when we just thumped the bad guys?"

"Progress," I said. "Modern technology. Onward and upward."

"Bullshit," Cowboy said.

"That, too," I said. "Especially that."

30

"Hello?"

"This is Colonel Sankowski," I said. "Put Archer on."

"Archer?" the voice said. "You must have—uh, wait a minute there. Right, Colonel. This is Archer."

"Are you available for work?"

"Archer," he said. "I nearly forgot, it's been so long. You get my name from that old ad?"

"Never mind that. Are you available or not?" Leave the sweet-talk to the IBM recruiters; we mercenary colonels are hard as nails. Rusty nails. *Aarrgh*.

The man who'd called himself Archer waited a moment, then said. "Maybe. Where?"

"Here. Domestic."

"Umm," he said.

"It's a solo penetration job," I said. "Not quite what you'd asked for, but—"

"Tell you what. If you want a soldier, I'm your man. Give me a platoon in El Sal, or Nicaragua, or anyplace else they got commies to kill, and I'll give you the highest body counts in the company. But don't try to blow smoke up my ass with this solo penetration shit. I don't do office burglaries. I don't break legs, either."

Then it was my turn to say, "Umm."

"So, Colonel, you got a platoon for me to lead? Or troops to train? I do weapons training, too."

"No," I said.

He hung up.

"I think we can take Archer off the list," I said to Cowboy.

31

Over the next few days I talked to eight of the seventeen possible hitters. Most of them seemed to be like Archer, former grunts who'd found they liked military life but were bored by peacetime soldiering.

They were surprisingly picky about the work they would accept. They all wanted overseas assignments. What they did was more important to them than what they got paid for doing it. They would fight for a government or for a revolutionary group, that didn't matter, but the politics of the conflict had to be correct. None of the men would, for any amount of money, contract with a procommunist regime or rebel group.

One of the eight, an explosives guy in Oklahoma, wasn't interested in mercenary work of any kind. "Shit, man," he said, "I ain't into that bullshit no more."

"This is domestic," I said. "No travel. And the pay's good."

"Naw, Colonel, I'm right out of it now."

"All the way out?"

"Depends on how you look at it, I s'pose." He laughed. It

wasn't a particularly jolly laugh. "I left both hands and one eye in fuckin' Angola, man. But what's left of me is all the way out." He laughed again, and he was still laughing when the phone clattered and went dead.

I scratched him off the list. Two down; cooking right along there, Rafferty. But they were the easy ones. They were still at their old phone numbers; all I had to do was call when they were home. In between those simple calls, I talked to other people. Oh, boy, did I talk to other people.

———

"Telephone company, subscriber records, may I help you?"

"Sure hope so. This is Dave Howdiston, at the Baton Rouge business office. Listen, I got a problem with a subscriber's records. New account for us, but he says he was one of yours a few years back."

"Yes?"

"Do you have this variable deposit plan up there? Well, we do, and I mean to tell you it is the … Anyway, the thing of it is, we have to get a telephone subscription credit history on all new accounts, right? So I had all that information for the subscriber I was telling you about, but the computer burped, or I pushed the wrong button or something. I don't know for sure it was my fault, but it probably was. I'm not too good with this thing. Anyway, almost everything is gone. Now all I can get on the screen is the old number up there in your neck of the woods. I can't even get the subscriber's name up, and I can't remember it, and he's supposed to have a touch-tone and three-way service, two extra jacks, and an extension bell installed by tomorrow. I'm in big trouble here."

"But I don t see what I can—"

"Way I figure it, your computer might show where the

subscriber went after his service was terminated with you. Where you sent the final bill, right? Then I can check there and see what records they have and keep doing that until I track him right back to the other side of my counter here."

"Well, I suppose that would work."

"I'll put you on my Christmas card list. Promise."

She chuckled. Nice chuckle. "Okay, okay. What was the subscriber's former number here?"

I gave her the phone number from the Dagger ad and the approximate date. Forty-five seconds later, she told me his name and forwarding address.

I said, "By golly, next time you come to Baton Rouge, pop into the business office at lunchtime and ask for Dave. I'm gonna buy you a big bowl of the best gumbo you ever tasted."

"Happy to help out. Bye now."

"So long." I hung up and said, "Bingo. Scottsdale, Arizona."

Cowboy shook his head slowly. "My, oh my," he said. "You surely do work at it."

———

During my telephone search for him, the hitter did not call about the money. Well, maybe he tried to call and couldn't get through. Hell with him. As long as I was making progress, I'd tie up my phone as much as I wanted.

———

"What is it?" Waspish male voice.

"This is Special Agent Preston," I said, "at the Federal Building. We have reason to believe one of your boxes may have been used for fraudulent purposes at one time."

"Your problem," he said. "My people just collect the rental and put the mail in the boxes. No skin off our necks. I can show you in the book where it says that, too."

"We're in absolute agreement there, Mr. Postmaster," I smarmed. The bastard hadn't even told me his name. "There is not a shadow of suspicion about anyone at your Post Office. Not a shadow. About anyone. However, for the purposes of a successful investigation, certain information would be—"

"Court order," he said.

"Pardon?"

"Court order. What are you, deaf? Get a court order if you want to see my box records."

"Well, I could do that, of course, but I thought we might save—"

"Saving's for banks, buster. This is a post office. Let me know when you've got your court order. I'm busy now. Good bye." He hung up.

"I hope your stamps fall off," I said to the dead phone.

We finally ran that one down, but not until I'd enlisted Ed Durkee's help and accumulated a stack of owed favors I couldn't jump over.

And after all that, the ad—it was the Occupant one—turned out to be a junior college criminology project to study *"Sub Rosa Recruiting Techniques in Modern America"*.

No kidding, this business can break your heart sometimes.

———

While I numbed my ear on the telephone, Cowboy cross-checked our ever-changing list against Dresden's telephone index and the printout of Ford Tempo registrations. We continued to strike out on both fronts.

———

One of the old ads had a Dallas phone number but no one ever seemed to be home. I dug around in my stack of old phone books and such, and came up with a Cole's reverse directory for the same year as the magazine ad. The phone number tied back to an address in northeast Dallas. The old Cole's said A. Cordington lived there then. This year's Cole's had ever better news: Cordington *still* lived there. Southwestern Bell's current book said so, too, but neither Cole's nor Ma Bell had any thoughts on why A. Cordington didn't answer his phone.

Cowboy looked up from the Tempo registration list. "He ain't in here," he said. "Or in Dresden's phone number doohickey, either."

"I'll keep trying him between other calls. And what the hell, this guy's a local. We can pull his chain any time we want."

———

I called Hilda Thursday. Well, I called her Wednesday night, but she hadn't spent a night alone then. By Thursday she had.

"Slept like a baby," she said.

"No nightmares?"

"No. I woke up once, about three-thirty, feeling a little uneasy. But I went right back to sleep."

"That's great, babe," I said. "But listen, you don't have to be so stalwart about *all* your nighttime problems. It's all right to admit that you couldn't sleep, you tossed and turned, and pined for the presence of my body."

"Slept like a baby," she said again. "Sorry."

The cat came around on Friday morning. It drank half a bowl of milk not ten feet from me, then eyed a leftover chicken leg I'd brought out for it. Cat wouldn't take the chicken leg out of my hand, but it finally sneaked up when I put the drumstick on the ground and pretended to look the other way. It was incredible how slowly the cat moved and how rigidly it froze into position when it thought I was peeking. When the cat picked up the piece of chicken, it trotted away, all bouncy and busy but still controlled. I could tell it wanted to run but it was too cool to do so.

Cat had a lot of class.

———

"This one isn't much for false modesty," I said to Cowboy on Friday. "Listen to this. 'Rugged, fearless, skilled.'"

"He ain't much for basic security, either. Imagine putting your name, address, and phone number in one of them ads."

"I'll mention that to rugged, fearless, and skilled Lee Forelander when I speak to him," I said.

The address was in Dayton, Ohio, which seemed a long way to commute to a Texas killing. But the ad was five years old and he might have moved since then, and besides, you have to start someplace.

Ten minutes later, I wished I hadn't left him until so late in the search.

I put down the phone and told Cowboy, "This one looks pretty good. Forelander doesn't live there anymore, but the woman I spoke to used to rent the house to Forelander and his family. Now get this. He's career Air Force, stationed at Wright-Patterson while he was there."

"Probably a pilot or something," Cowboy said.

"Not according to his old landlady. She says he's an MP."

"Promising," Cowboy said. "That sounds downright promising."

The Wright-Patterson base security office remembered Forelander and suggested I try Travis Air Force Base. The voice at Wright-Pat was pretty goosey about giving out that kind of information, so when I phoned Travis, I stayed away from the higher, more inquisitive, levels of the system.

"Yes, sir, I remember Sergeant Forelander," an airman on duty at the base post office said. "I didn't know him person-ally, but I saw him beat Major Cavanagh by eleven points last year. And that was after Major Cavanagh had been base champion for three years straight. It was very exciting."

Wonderful, I thought. I'm trying to find a killer, and this guy wants to chat about bowling. "Imagine that," I said. "Would you have his home address handy, maybe a phone number?"

"It's probably in the files, sir. I'll check." While he looked, he rambled on about that stupid bowling tournament. "Most of us didn't know Sergeant Forelander, so we were surprised when he made the finals. Then he won. By eleven points, wow. Major Cavanagh was really steamed, but that's the way it goes, right? The major's good, but Sergeant Forelander was better. The best, probably. I don't think I've ever seen anyone shoot like—aha, here we are. Sergeant Forelander isn't stationed here at Travis anymore, I guess you know that, but—"

"Wait a minute. Shoot?"

"Yes, sir. I just told you. Sergeant Forelander won the base pistol shoot last year. Is this phone all right today? Because sometimes it—"

"It's fine," I said. "A memorable phone. Go ahead with the address, please."

"Right." He sounded puzzled but still friendly. He read out a phone number. "That area code is 817, sir."

"Fort Worth is area 817," I said. "Good old 817."

"Um, believe you're right, sir."

"A perfect phone," I said. "One of the great phones of all time."

"Yes, sir," he said. "Is there anything else I can do for you?" He didn't sound like he wanted me to say yes. I didn't. We hung up.

I told Cowboy what I'd learned and said, "Forelander is probably stationed at Carswell. How's that for handy? A fast run across on the freeway, down Walnut Hill Lane, pop Max in the back of the head, and back to the guardhouse before you can say 'Let me see your security pass.'"

Cowboy stopped flipping through the Tempo registrations and said, "I 'spect I oughta make the next call, then."

"Yeah, he might recognize my voice. Try to hire him for something; set up a meet, anywhere he'll go for. Hot damn, I think this is it."

I got two beers from the refrigerator and handed Cowboy one while he called the Forelander number in Fort Worth. I paced back and forth twice, then thought to check the Fort Worth phone book. Lee Forelander wasn't listed, but that didn't mean much. What with a recent transfer and all ...

"Howdy," Cowboy said, "Lee Forelander, please."

After that Cowboy's side of the conversation was mostly "Um-hmm," and "Yes'm," and "Do tell."

We're on a roll, I thought.

Then Cowboy said to the phone, "It probably don't matter now, ma'am, but I'm calling about an ad he—"

Uh-oh, I thought.

Back to "Ums," and "How 'bout that," and "Ain't it the truth." Cowboy began to grin and shake his head ruefully.

Aw, shit, I thought.

With some justification, as it turned out.

"Okay," Cowboy said when he'd hung up. "Here's the story. Mama's kind of a talker, so I found out lots more than we need to know."

"Or want to know, I suspect."

He nodded. "That's so. Anyhow, there's two of 'em. Airman First Lee Forelander and Sergeant Lee Forelander; a boy and his daddy. But ain't neither one of them stationed at Carswell like we thought. The sergeant—he's the pistol shooter—he's been freezing his butt off at Thule. In Greenland, you know. Four months temporary duty. The boy, the airman, he works on cruise missiles. He's been in England for a year, his mama says, 'where all those horrible women are outside the base,' and she hopes he don't meet one of them and catch anything,"

"Who put the ad in the magazine?"

"The kid. He was in high school then, having the usual growin'-up hassles with his folks. Miz Forelander thinks the young'un was trying to impress his daddy. You know how kids are. It got to be a family joke, she says. He got a coupla calls way back then, not that he did anything about them. When I mentioned it just now, that was the first time she'd thought of it for years." Cowboy shrugged. "Too bad. It looked real good for a little while there."

"Well, goddamn," I said.

———

As Friday lurched into the weekend, the list of possibles steadily shortened. Some people we found and talked to.

Others led us up blind alleys, or their trails grew cold and barren in distant cities. When that happened, we asked ourselves if we'd followed them farther than Dresden would have. If we had, we quit there and called it even. If we hadn't, we stuck with it.

Southwestern Bell announced record profits for the quarter and increased dividends, but that was probably only a coincidence. Probably.

Between working the other leads, I kept circling back to my own telephonic backyard and listening to A. Cordington's phone ring.

I had come to think of him as my ace in the hole. No matter how the others worked out, I always had good old A. Cordington handy. If he wouldn't answer his phone, I could always go to him.

Except, way in the background, there was the nagging worry that Cordington would turn out to be clean, too.

And if they were all clean, I was in big trouble, because I didn't know what to try next.

By one-thirty on Saturday afternoon, we had shaved the list down to three. There was Cordington; Striker, who had left a Montreal forwarding address at a Baltimore boarding-house eighteen months ago; and a Kansas City phone number we were almost ready to abandon as a lost cause.

I called Cordington for what seemed like the seventy-third time.

"Hello?" someone said.

32

"Hel-lo-o-o?" the voice said again. It was a woman.

"Uh, right," I said. "Hello."

"I think we're finished with that part," she said. "Now what shall we talk about?"

"Right," I said again, and scrabbled on the coffee table for the magazine with the right ad in it. I'd tried the Cordington number unsuccessfully so many times, I'd forgotten who he was supposed to be. Or who *I* was supposed to be.

"This is Colonel Sandowski," I said. I almost said Colonel Sanders, for god's sake. "Put Eagle on."

She sighed a sharp, disgusted sigh. "Again?" she snapped. "How many times do I have to tell you? Play your dumb Eagle games if you want but leave me out of it. I'm working the worst block on the roster; I *walked* every inch of the way from Chicago to D-FW this morning, and you expect me to— oh, go to hell." She hung up with a noisy rattle and a final click.

Cowboy looked at me with a sleepy question on his face. I slowly hung up my phone and extended my open hands in a broad see-how-easy-that-was gesture. "Ta-da!" I said.

Cowboy stood up and stretched. "'Bout time," he said. "Let's go git him."

———

Twenty-seven minutes later, we got out of the Mustang in front of A. Cordington's address. It was one of a hundred or more apartments in a complex that sprawled across a rolling site off Greenville Avenue. The apartments were built in two- and four-unit blocks, with no building taller than two stories. The complex had a fancy name with Crest or Creek or Glen in it. Maybe all three; I'd already forgotten it.

The area was fairly new, well landscaped, clean, and aggressively healthy. On the way in, we had passed a glass-walled building full of exercise equipment, and two Olympic pools. Joggers in headbands and bright clothes grinned and sweated along the winding drives. The carports were bright with RX-7s, Fieros, and small BMWs. The place looked like an outdoor set for *Thirtysomething*.

"Welcome to level one of yuppie nirvana," I said. "From here on, it only gets more glitzy."

Cowboy shook his head. "It don't do nothing for me. Ain't no horses, far as I can see."

Cordington lived in a single-story two-unit building, in the apartment on the left. I pushed the doorbell. Chimes bonged inside.

Nothing happened for two or three minutes, then the door to the other apartment opened. A young woman in her early twenties came out. She was short, busty, pretty, with red hair and a button nose. She wore spotless, perhaps ironed, high-cut jogging shorts and a Hash House Harriers tank top. She said, "Oh, hey, guys, I think Tony is still— Whoops, I tell a lie."

She pointed to a yellow Honda Prelude in the carport. "Silly me." She looked Cowboy up and down, smiled, and waggled her fingers at him. "Bye." When she walked away, she waggled her butt at him. At the curb she began to jog. That was pretty interesting, too.

Cowboy watched her go, then said to me, "I flat don't understand it. Don't you reckon all that bouncin' and floppin' would *hurt*?"

Before I could agree, the Cordington door opened. Another woman, slightly older and taller, stood with one hand on the doorknob. She wore a full-length white terry cloth robe and had a towel wrapped turban-fashion around her hair. Her face was scrubbed and pink. She said, "I think I made a big mistake opening this door."

I grinned at her; gave her my absolute best winning smile. "Hi," I said. "We'd like to talk to Tony."

It occurred to me that I should have sent Cowboy to cover the back. Cordington could be crawling out a bedroom window while we stooged around at the front door.

The robed woman looked confused. "Go ahead," she said.

Then I began to get confused. "Tony Cordington," I said. "Eagle. He put an ad in a magazine ..." Weak, Rafferty, weak.

She rolled her eyes and said, "Was that you on the phone? Look, *I'm* Tony Cordington. Antonia; Tony, get it?"

Well, damn! I said, "That sound you hear is me kicking myself."

She frowned. "The sound you hear is me deciding whether to call the cops or slam this door in your face or both."

"Two things to consider, Tony. One: this is important. Whoever Eagle is, I'm going to find him. It will be easier on all of us, especially him, if you help me. Two: if you do help me, we'll go away, not come back, and I'll keep you out of the official part of it. Oh, hey, I just thought of a third thing." I showed her my winning smile again. "Would a face like this lie to you?"

After ten seconds she shrugged and stepped aside. "I'm messing up," she said. "I know I'm messing up, but this one I gotta hear."

I don't care what Hilda says, the old Rafferty smile gets 'em every time.

Tony Cordington waved us ahead into her living room, toward two beige leather sofas with a glass coffee table between them. She hung back, though, and when we turned around, she held up a small black aerosol can.

"You guys sit down," he said, "and tell me what's going on. But first let me tell you something. The biggest, meanest man in Dallas lives right across the street. He and his shotgun will be here in two seconds if I set off this siren gadget." She put the aerosol alarm back in her robe pocket, left her hand in there, too, and leaned against the open front door. "So talk," she said.

"You got it." I sprawled on her sofa and committed an unnatural act. I told her the truth.

Not the whole truth, of course. I skipped the part about Eagle killing Max Krandorff. I thought Tony might be more willing to point me toward her friend—or whatever he was to her—if she didn't know that we knew that he … anyway, it seemed like a good idea.

But for once I was too cynical. Almost from the beginning, it was obvious Tony Cordington was learning all this for the first time. She grimaced when I told her about the almost-fire-bomb and shook her head when I mentioned how bleary Eagle had sounded in his last phone call. "He's running, Tony. And he's running down, too. Pretty soon he'll do something stupid and someone will get hurt. It might be him."

Tony Cordington stood with her shoulders slumped and her head down. She took her alarm hand out of her pocket—empty—and used the heel of it to rub her eyes. "The poor damn fool," she said.

"Do you know where he is?" I said.

"Oh, sure."

"Will you tell me?"

"Yes."

33

Tony Cordington came away from her front door and dropped onto the sofa beside me. I moved to the sofa opposite; I wanted to watch her while she told me about Eagle.

She stretched a long arm out along the sofa back and looked at the end wall. She bit her lip and made a sharp clicking sound with her tongue. She blinked a lot, too. She was holding back the tears, but it wasn't easy.

I said, "This probably doesn't help much, but you're doing the right thing, Why don't you start with his name?"

She nodded jerkily four or five times, then said in a low voice, "His name is Bert Cannon. He's really a very decent guy, but ..."

"Where does he live?"

She shook her head. "I don't know."

"Tony, it's no use—"

She glared at me and said, very deliberately, "I am not protecting him. I do not know where Bert lives."

The question was too obvious to need asking, so I just waited. When she had finished glaring at me, she developed a great interest in the seam along the back of the sofa. Finally she said to the seam, "There's this store in Richardson called Moretins. On Jupiter Road. It's a, oh, you know, an outdoor store."

"Tents, sleeping bags," I said.

She nodded. "And packs and boots and ropes and things. Bert works there. That's what I meant when I said I knew where he is."

"That's fine, Tony. Thank you."

"Can I tell you more about him, before you go aft—before you leave?"

"Sure," I said.

She scootched to the edge of the sofa and leaned forward, with her elbows on her knees and her hands clasped in front of her. "I've known Bert Cannon for years and years, almost as long as I can remember," she said. "We grew up on the same block in Abilene. I had a crush on Bert when I was nine. He was seventeen then. An older man, swoon, swoon. Pretty dumb, eh?

"Even with him being so much older, because we lived so close, I saw Bert around a lot. He was always so kind to me. He was the only boy I knew who would listen. He wouldn't laugh or tease me. He'd *listen* to me. You probably don't know how important that is to a young girl. That, and the way I felt so mature and grown-up when I talked with Bert." She smiled a little and mock-grimaced. "God, this is embarrassing! Important, though. It won't kill me. Well, Bert has always been freaky about guns and soldiers and all that."

She saw Cowboy and me look at each other, and her eyes opened wider. "No, no," she said. "Don't get the wrong idea! He wasn't mean or a bully or anything like that. He liked to hunt, that's all—everybody in Abilene liked to hunt, I think— and he planned to join the marines. He wanted to be a marine so badly, and he wanted to go to Vietnam. It was really strange. Other boys talked about how terrible the war was and how they'd go to Canada to beat the draft and all that, but Bert had this huge Marine Corps recruiting poster on his bedroom wall. Anyway, Bert went to junior college first—his parents insisted—then he joined up. In time for Vietnam, too. Just barely, but in time, if everything had worked out for him.

"It didn't, though," she said. "During basic training, on the rifle range, another recruit did something wrong. They have these rules, you know, about handling the guns, but this other guy messed up, and Bert got shot in the foot. They had to amputate one entire toe and most of another one. You'd never know it, except he walks a little funny when he's tired. It was bad enough, though. The same week Bert got out of the hospital, the Marine Corps discharged him. It nearly broke Bert's heart."

Cowboy murmured, "Don't know about the marines, but the army used to have problems with that. Some old boys managed to get themselves shot in the foot deliberate-like. To get out."

Tony shook her head firmly. "No way! Not Bert. In fact, he worried himself sick that people might think that. He appealed to some government board or committee or something, trying to get back into the marines, but it didn't work. He wrote to his congressman, too. Fat lot of good that did." She shrugged. "He even tried to join the army, too, starting from scratch. Because of his toes, he couldn't pass the physical.

"Bert stayed with his folks, there in Abilene, while he tried all those things. We talked a lot. I was still pretty young. Eleven or twelve, I guess, but we got along amazingly well. Then he left. Came here, to Dallas. I was sorry to see him go, but I was over that crush by then. We were friends, that's all."

She snorted softly. "How many times have you heard that one? Just friends. It was true, though. Then, anyway. After he left, we didn't even write to each other very much. Oh, at first we did, or I did anyway, but then … a card at Christmas, that's about all."

She pressed her hands against her knees and arched her back. "So, Bert was gone. I finished growing up and eventually did the junior college thing, too, and right after graduation I lucked into this job with the airline. Before you know it —boom boom, I'm in Dallas, too. Mr. and Mrs. Cannon wrote to Bert about it. One day he knocked on the door and it was like … well, it was wonderful to see him, but it was sure different. And better! We'd known each other for years, but that was the first time ever when we were both adults."

She smiled fondly. "Two weeks later, Bert moved in here. We lived together for almost three years."

She didn't say any more after that. The silence had stretched out for several minutes when I finally said, "What happened?"

She dropped her head and looked at her hands. "Bert began to change. Or maybe he had already changed, but I didn't see it at first." Her shoulders slumped a little more, and she said. "You remember, I told you how disappointed he was when the Marine Corps wouldn't let him stay in? Well, he never really got over that. He was almost compulsive about being a soldier. He bought all kinds of magazines about soldiers and mercenaries and all that stuff. He went to a convention one year, out West somewhere. When he came back, he was all worked up. He said he'd talked to people about where to get mercenary jobs. He was finally going to be a soldier."

She sniffed loudly. "But that didn't work out for Bert, either. He wrote letters, and he phoned people, and he went to join up or apply or whatever mercenary soldiers do, but no one wanted him. He didn't have any military experience. So poor Bert couldn't be a pretend soldier because he'd never been a real soldier. It didn't seem fair."

Cowboy squirmed when she said "pretend soldier," but before he could say anything, I jumped in. "Then Bert only claimed to have been a marine in his ad, so he'd have a better shot at a merc contract."

Tony nodded. "Yes. And that ad was the last straw for me. I had tried to help him get over that … that *need* to be a soldier. It was crazy! Well, not crazy-crazy, I don't mean that, but crazy-odd, right? And why? That's what I could never figure out. Why? He had a decent job; he got a little money from Veterans Affairs; he was old enough to settle down and stop pipe dreaming about being a mercenary in Africa or wherever. Then he sent in that stupid ad. Eagle, for crying out loud." She shook her head sadly.

I said, "Did many people answer it?"

"Some. Nothing worthwhile, nothing like what he wanted. I think he expected a great big tank to pick him up out front. He cleaned his guns over and over, and he started wearing those funny clothes on weekends; the blotchy brown-and-green ones. Ah, camouflage, that's it."

"I think they call them cammies now."

"That's right! The first time he said that, I thought he said 'jammies,' and I wondered why he was going to put on his pajamas at five o'clock."

"So no one hired him?"

"No. The poor guy was so disappointed. He started drinking too much, and I was already mad about that stupid ad, so when I came home from a terrible, stinking flight and Bert was here with a guy he'd met in a bar, and it was so *obvious* the jerk was stringing Bert along, that I …"

The memory of it still bothered her. She rubbed her eyes with both hands and said between her wrists, "I told Bert to get out. I was sick to death of smelling dumb old gun oil and listening to him talk about this battle and that revolution." She lowered her hands and looked at me with reddened eyes. "He wore me out. I swear, he just plain wore me out. I was so tired of seeing him fool himself. I wasn't angry. I loved him. I still do, a little bit anyway. But I couldn't take it anymore. We had a good cry, both of us, and he moved out the next morning. I told him to come back when he got over his problem. That was five years ago. He hasn't come back."

"But you took a phone call for him recently, and passed the message on, didn't you?" Shows you the benefit of being a trained detective. When someone paints the obvious in bright red letters and underlines it and dots the I's with flashing lights, hey, I notice it right off the bat.

Tony said, "Uh-huh. I was going to tell the man on the phone to get lost; then I thought, it's a perfect test. After five years, if Bert can ignore this, maybe he can make it. So I called Bert at the store and told him. He phoned me back the next day, absolutely berserk with goofy plans. He was going to take this job: whatever it was, and make a zillion dollars. The money would let him buy land down in the Piney Woods, he said, and he would start a training camp for mercenary soldiers. He'd teach them jungle warfare and survival and I don't know what all." She shook her head, saddened, but dry-eyed about it now. "He sounded worse than ever."

I said, "Tony, I didn't tell you everything before. Bert is getting worse, all right. He's up to dangerous now. The man you talked to hired Bert to kill his business partner."

"No!" Her eyes were huge.

"Yes. And Bert took the job. And the partner is dead."

She shook her head, slowly but positively. "Bert did not

kill him. I cannot believe that. He gets carried away, sure, and he's pretty silly about this soldier thing, but ... never, not in million years."

"You understand, though, that if I'm right—take it easy, I said *if*—it's still better for Bert to be out of circulation."

"I understand that," she said, "but you're wrong. Bert wouldn't kill anyone."

"Well ..."

Her face creased in a sudden frown. "You're not going to let the police go after him, are you?"

"Tony, the police have to be involved here. Whether you think so or not, Bert's wanted for—"

"No," she said sharply, "I don't mean that! I know the police will have to hold him, at least for a while, until they find out he didn't do it. The thing is, I want *you* to take Bert to the police. Why do you think I told you all those personal things?"

"But—"

"You know about Bert now. Real cops, sorry, um, ordinary cops won't realize what his problem is. They might shoot him if he did something foolish." She looked from me to Cowboy; her face anxious. "Please?"

Cowboy gave me a look that said he, too, would shoot Bert if he did anything foolish, so what else was new? But he shrugged and said, "It don't make no never-mind to me."

"If we can," I told Tony. I'd halfway planned on it anyway, what with Kevin Noonebury gumming up the works. "Do have a picture of him?"

"Oh, sure. Hang on."

———

Five minutes later, as we climbed into the Mustang, I said to Cowboy, "When it happens, let's give the silly bastard a break, if we can."

Cowboy snorted. "They ain't a whole lot we can do about it," he said. "It depends on good old Bert. However we bring him back, laughing or bleeding or cold dead meat, it's all up to him."

34

"Got him," Cowboy said, looking up from the list of Ford Tempo registrations. "Bertram L. Cannon. Address out in Mesquite. It looks like an apartment house."

"Well, well," I said.

The phone rang. Ed Durkee's voice said, "I knew if I gave you that damned cellular phone, I'd regret it." I had chased him down at home twenty-five minutes earlier.

Now he said, "The first Saturday in months that we've had people over and ... anyway, Cannon has form but nothing serious. He got picked up for drunk-and-disorderly two and a half years ago. A bar fight. He pleaded guilty and paid his fine. Officially he is now a model citizen."

"Hey—"

"Think about it, Rafferty. If we had Dresden, and if Dresden had confessed, I'd have Cannon by the balls. But I don't. And the firebomb thing at your house won't wash. You didn't ever see him."

"The phone calls?"

"Aw, come on. You know better than that. Can you see me

trying to convince one of those smart-ass assistant DAs to bring a charge on that? First thing they're gonna ask is, how can Rafferty testify the calls came from the defendant? They're gonna say: 'What is he, a walking voiceprint machine?'"

Ed grunted. "And that's assuming I could keep Noonebury's troops from hearing about it and stealing the case away. Which I doubt. Look, I'm sorry as hell, but there isn't enough here to work with. Yet. Officially." He stopped talking. Way in the background on his end of the line, a child screamed happily. Then Ed said, "So what are you going to do?"

"I might give him a call. Maybe he'd like to meet me in your office Monday morning, nine sharp, to confess."

"Yeah, you could try that," Ed said.

"Or maybe I should snatch him off the street and sweat him until he comes up with hard evidence even a DA can underst—"

"Goddamned phone's gone dead again," Ed said. "I gotta get this fixed some day." He hung up.

I hung up, too, and turned to Cowboy, lounging on my sofa with a beer in one hand. "Care to sample the fleshpots of Mesquite?"

Cowboy nodded and levered himself upright. "Something gonna go wrong," he said. "Whenever you get all chirpy like that, by God, something goes wrong."

"No way!"

"Wait for it," he said.

———

Mesquite is a small city on the southeast side of what the Chamber of Commerce likes to call the Dallas Metroplex.

Mesquite is like most cities; it has good parts and bad

parts. Where Bert Cannon lived was in-between, slowly slipping toward bad. It was a boardinghouse, not apartments; it had been there a long time and it showed every decade.

"There's his car," Cowboy said. I parked the Mustang thirty yards away, where we could watch both the Tempo and the front door of the white frame building.

"How you want to play this?" Cowboy said. "Me, I ain't too whipped up about dragging him out of no third floor room if he don't want to come. That's an old building. Probably got cardboard walls. He decides to hole up and shoot, It's gonna be hard on folks up, down, either side of him."

"Let's sit tight for a while. It's, what, six-thirty on a Saturday night? He'll probably be going out soon. We'll grab him then."

But he didn't, so we couldn't, and we sat there, bored out of our skulls, for the next six hours. I kept Cannon's picture propped up on the dashboard. No one like him entered or left the building. "Told you this wouldn't be easy," Cowboy said.

At midnight I left Cowboy standing under a tree and I went looking for food. Fifteen minutes later, I was back with a bag of McDonald's finest. We dined *alfresco*, hunkered down well back in the tree shadows. Hot tip for gracious living: Hamburgers under a tree in the small dark hours will never replace real picnics. Trust me on that one.

"Don't even know if he's in there," Cowboy said. "He might have walked, or gone away with somebody in their car."

"'Stake out the suspect's house or car or both,'" I said. "'Eventually they will return.' I distinctly remember highlighting that part in my *Philip Marlowe Crime Fighter Manual*."

Cowboy grunted. "Hilda's right. You are weird sometimes."

By the time we could reasonably assume Bert Cannon was

either in for the night or wouldn't be back till tomorrow, it was tomorrow. Too late to go home, get any sleep, and be back for an early start. So we slept in the car. Well, we took turns trying to sleep in the car.

At six a.m., I leaned against the tree while Cowboy scrounged the wilds of Mesquite for food. And so the day began, with bitter coffee, doughnuts, scratching, and a personal grimy feeling. Welcome to Sunday morning. I much preferred Sundays at Hilda's, with icy Ramos gin fizzes, platters of grazing food, and Garrick and Maria on the kitchen television set.

At seven-seventeen Cannon came out of his building. He was a little shorter than I'd thought he'd be, but chunkier. He had a mustache, a close-cropped, military-style haircut, and a purposeful, in-control-and-loving-it stride.

"Tony was right," I said. "You'd never know he has a shot-up foot."

"Early in the day," Cowboy said. "And he only walked fifty feet. I bet he don't step out like that halfway through a twenty-mile forced march."

"Who does?"

Cannon unlocked the Tempo, got in, and led us away to downtown Mesquite. He parked in front of a coffee shop, bought a paper from a dispenser, and went inside slowly, scanning the headlines.

"I didn't have him pegged for the power-breakfast type," I said.

"He ain't," Cowboy said. "He's the hot-plate-in-his-room, too-much-trouble-to-cook type."

Cowboy got out and followed Cannon into the coffee shop. I made a quick sweep through the alley behind the building, on the off chance he'd made us. There was no sign of him, though, so I parked near the corner, then pawed through the cluttered backseat, looking for … inspiration, I guess.

Cannon had apparently seen me take the money from Dresden, so it seemed a good idea to disguise myself. Nothing fancy, just enough to confuse him momentarily; let me get close enough to short-circuit a Shoot-Out In The OK Coffee Shop.

I found a crumpled straw western hat and a tarnished pair of mirrored sunglasses mixed in with the other backseat junk. Close enough. I put them on and walked around to the coffee shop. The sunglasses were scratched and smeared, hard to see through.

The coffee shop was about half-full. Two or three people sat empty-faced over coffee cups, but most of the customers were deep in their Sunday papers. Cannon sat on a stool at a long counter along the right-hand wall. He held his paper in his left hand and mechanically sipped coffee with his right. Ten feet behind his left shoulder Cowboy sat alone at a table for two.

There was an empty space at the counter two stools this side of Cannon, where a large man in an electric-blue leisure suit would be between me and Bert. I took that stool, nodded when the waitress held up a coffee cup and watched her slop a third of it into the saucer before she plunked it down in front of me. Sunday brunch at the Hilton this was not.

I wanted to let Cannon settle in for a few minutes, but the guy in the leisure suit started the clock early when he abruptly backed off his stool and walked away. Good-bye, screen. I got up then and stepped closer to Cannon. I felt Cowboy moving in from the other side. I dropped money onto the counter in front of Cannon. He jumped, startled, and I grabbed his right arm above the elbow where you can clamp down hard and make the whole arm go numb.

Cowboy had Bert's left arm by then, and we lifted him off his stool, moved him along, always a half-step off-balance, and waltzed him right on out of there. A few heads came up out of newspapers and watched us, but no one said or did anything,

We were outside on the sidewalk, still bustling him along, before Bert seemed to realize what was happening. He started to complain then, but its not easy to take control of a situation when your arms don't work and two large men are treating you like a piece of furniture.

At the Mustang, we patted him down. He was clean, so we shoved him into the trunk and drove away. I looked in the rearview mirror. There didn't seem to be anyone writing down my license plate number or rushing to get the cops.

Picking up Bert Cannon was anticlimactic, to tell you the truth. I felt cheated. Not so cheated that I wanted to throw him back and try again, but a little bit cheated.

35

"Fuck you guys," Cannon said. "I got nothing to say. You got me. Okay, I accept that. You took me by surprise, that's all. Doesn't mean you're tougher than I am. No goddamned way. I'll show you jerk-offs who's the tough one around here. You'll see. In the Corps, we learned how to hang tough. You think I'm gonna tell you *anything*, why … Hey, I'll tell you this much. You're shit out of luck. S.O.L. Believe it. Go on, try me. You'll see. I got nothing to say. Not me. Nothing."

All that started after he'd realized we weren't cops and my house wasn't the local police station. He'd been repeating himself for five minutes now, and showed no signs of slowing down as he stood in the middle of my living room.

Cowboy and I stood back away from him, covering the room exits without making it obvious. Cannon didn't bolt, didn't even walk around. He just stood there and bitched. Boring.

Cowboy sat down on the couch; I leaned against a chair. I half turned away from Cannon and said to Cowboy, "So what do you think of the Cowboys' chances this year?"

"I reckon the key to it is fan support," he said solemnly. "If the town don't really get out there and back the team, you can't expect 'em to win."

Cannon spluttered to a halt when he realized we weren't listening to him. He folded his arms and scowled. The silence made a delightful contrast.

"Take off your clothes," I said to Cannon over my shoulder and to Cowboy, "Have you seen Harry's new Grand Prix? Fantastic. Now that's what I call—"

"Blow it out your ass," Cannon said.

I looked at Cowboy. He shrugged.

"Strip," I said to Cannon. "Yeah, the upholstery is this plush-looking—"

"What are you guys, a couple of queers or something? Forget it! I will not—"

"The hard way," I said to Cowboy.

"Looks like it," he said.

As we moved toward Cannon, he dropped into a fight stance and threw a long, looping swing at me. His arm was still a trifle numb, probably. In any case, it was easy to pick his right hand out of the air and gentle him down with a come-along hold. While I held his wrist bent down—as long as he didn't struggle, it wouldn't hurt him—Cowboy started unbuttoning and unsnapping his clothes.

"Tell you the truth," Cowboy said, "I kind of like the new Fords myself."

"Naw. Ford hasn't made a car worth having since the Mustang."

To get Cannon's shirt off, we switched. Cowboy bent Cannon left wrist for a change while I finished undressing him. Cannon bitched some in the beginning, but by the time he was down to his shorts—and about to lose those—he shut up.

"Ford makes good pickups," Cowboy said.

"Well, I dunno about that, but I'll tell you what. Ford paint doesn't last as long as GM's, everybody knows that."

I threw the last of Cannon's clothes into a corner. Cowboy looked at Cannon like he was a side of beef and sniffed. "Phew," he said, "Shower."

Cannon bleated. "Hey, c'mon! You saying I smell? I don't—"

He was right; he didn't. But being clean had nothing to do it.

"You're wrong about Ford paint. My cousin had him a LTD that—"

We trundled Cannon into the bathroom, turned on the water, and set the temperature. He tried to pull away, so I squeezed down harder on his upper arm. He winced but stopped pulling. I eased off the pressure but kept holding his arm. He let me steer him into the tub and under the shower head. He stood there like an animal in the rain, head bowed, his hair plastered down over his forehead. He trembled slightly. I noticed the wound Tony had mentioned. No wonder he couldn't get into the armed forces. That foot was a mess.

"A fluke," I said to Cowboy. "You can't beat GM cars for keeping a shine."

I handed Cannon a bar of soap. He didn't take it at first, so I pulled his arm out straight and began to wash it. While I scrubbed, I looked back at Cowboy and continued to slander Ford paint.

Cowboy shook his head and kept saying, "Naw, naw, you're wrong ..."

Tentatively, Cannon reached his free hand around, palm up. I put the soap into it. He began to wash himself.

I stepped back, dried my hands, and said, "Actually, you might be right about Ford pickups. I seem to recall an old ..."

Cowboy and I stood around beside the open shower, rambling on about this and that until Cannon finished washing himself and put the soap in the dish.

"I'm telling you, that brother-in-law of mine—" I pointed at Cannon's left knee. He got the soap out of the dish and washed his knee again. "—is gonna keep my lawn mower forever, it looks like. That son of a ..."

When he'd finished washing again, Cannon took the towel the first time Cowboy handed it to him. He dried himself quickly, then awkwardly folded the towel and hung it over the shower curtain rod. He started to step out of the tub, but Cowboy threw a hard glance at him, and he froze. We let him stand there for a few minutes, then led him out of the bathroom. He came quietly enough. I began to think it was going to work.

After that we locked Bert Cannon in a closet, ate breakfast and took turns napping.

Six hours later, when I let Cannon out, he was ready to talk.

36

"I didn't kill him," Cannon said. He sat awkwardly on a hard wooden chair in my kitchen, still naked, his legs crossed at the knee and his hands cupped over his crotch. "I swear to you, I didn't kill the old guy." It was the fourth time he'd denied killing Max Krandorff. Maybe it was true. And maybe not.

"You were hired to kill him," I said.

"Yes. Yes, that's right," he said, his head bobbing up and down. "But I didn't."

Cowboy, standing behind him, said, "Again. From the beginning."

Cannon nodded again. "All right. I'd been trying to get set up as a mercenary, but you have to have the right contacts and—" He stopped, then started again. "No one wanted me. That's the real truth of it. I'd never been a merc; I was only a marine for a few weeks before that bast— anyway, no one wanted me as a merc."

That was an improvement over his earlier, self-serving explanations. It would be interesting to see if anything else changed this time around.

"I'd almost forgotten that old ad, like I told you before. Then Tony called me at the store one day and said a man had—"

"When was that?" I said.

"Sorry. Okay, that was, uh, two and a half weeks ago. On a Thursday. Two weeks ago last Thursday."

"Go ahead."

"Tony said a man had called about the old Eagle ad. I don't know where he saw it. Well, in the magazine, sure, but where he found one that old, I don't know. Anyway, the guy left a number, Tony gave it to me, and I called him back."

I'd asked him about that phone number three times already. It was Dresden's home number. I let him go on with his story.

"He said his name was Carl, but he wouldn't tell me his last name," Cannon said. "He didn't come right out and say so, not at first, but he made it pretty clear that he wanted me to kill a guy named Max who worked in a grocery store—one of those late-night places. It looks like a barn."

I thought: Great security, Carl. Don't tell him your last name, but leave your home phone number. And a message. And then ask a strange voice on the phone to kill your partner. You dummy.

Cannon looked worried. "You have to understand this: I never intended to actually do it. But this Carl person offered me fifteen thousand dollars, and I thought … You see, for a long time I had this dream about buying a few hundred acres in east Texas. In the Piney Woods, maybe, or down in the Big Thicket. With that fifteen thousand and a little I've got saved, I'd have a down payment. What I wanted to do, see, was start a school where mercs—"

"You're kidding yourself again. Haven't you figured that out yet?"

He blinked and slowly said, "I'm beginning to." He rubbed his nose, then quickly dropped his hand back into his lap. "Well, I figured I could fool this guy Carl. He was uptight about the whole thing; that was pretty obvious. So I could pretend to kill this guy Max. What I'd really do, though, was take Max away, someplace where it would take him a couple of days to get back to Dallas. By then I'd have collected the money from Carl and"—Cannon shrugged—"what could he do about it? Go to the cops and say he was cheated because I hadn't murdered somebody for him?"

"When did you meet Carl the first time?"

Cannon shook his head. "I keep telling you, I *didn't* meet him. Not ever. See, we were supposed to meet downtown once. That was the Tuesday after he called. I told him where and what time but he never showed up. I waited for a whole hour, too. I don't know what happened to him—"

I did; Dresden went to the wrong place and met me instead.

"—but it seemed like someone else was trying to horn in, because when I called him that night, he didn't make much sense. He acted like I should have known things he'd never told me, and, well, it was weird."

I bet it was, with Carl and Bert talking at cross-purposes, confusing each other every time they opened their mouths. You could sell the film rights to a conversation like that: The Two Stooges Meet Ma Bell.

Cannon said, "And he kept saying things like, 'Remember, it's changed. Tomorrow night, not Thursday.' But he had never said anything about Thursday in the first place. He said he'd meet me afterward and pay me. And he said Wednesday, not Thursday, again. Why Thursday? I didn't know anything about Thursday. It was a little freaky."

"Don't you fret about that," Cowboy said softly. "It don't matter which day you iced him."

"But I *didn't* ice him! God, you guys, you gotta believe that. I went to the barn place Wednesday night, I admit that. I was there, okay? But it was *closed*. I couldn't get in."

He looked and acted nervous. "See, I had it all worked out. I was going to pretend to be drunk, right? Stagger some, talk funny, fake the old guy out. Then I'd grab him and lock him in the back room or the chiller or whatever had a door. Because if this Carl was going to meet me there, I couldn't take Max away like I'd planned at first. But I could lock him up, right? Maybe tie him up. I'd do whatever seemed like the best idea at the time. And then I'd tell Carl not to go into the store because of all the blood, or because he'd leave finger-prints or something. I figured I could snow him one way or another."

How's that for a professional, precisely organized *modus operandi*? Funny thing is, it might have worked.

"But I couldn't get in!" Cannon wailed. "Honest to God, I didn't kill the old guy!"

"How do you know he was old?"

"How many times do I have to tell you?" Cannon sounded desperate. "That Carl, on the phone, when he was acting weird, he told me. About sixty, he said. Kinda short, and bald."

"That's not much of a description."

Cannon slumped. "You don't bel— Max was supposed to be the only person in the store. How could I go wrong?"

"I don't know," I said. "Where *did* you go wrong? Did he try to fight? Bert, we understand about these things. You didn't mean to hurt him when you went in. Okay. We under-stand that. But maybe he struggled. He might have screamed; maybe he hit you, I don't know. Whatever it was, you got excited and things went further than you'd planned. Hey, it happens."

"But it didn't happen! Honest to God. The doors were locked, and I couldn't get in. There was a sign. Cleaning, it said. I kicked the door and yelled for the old guy, but he *never came to the door!*"

"Let's skip that for now," I said. "What happened next?"

"I didn't know what to do, except leave. I drove around for a while, killing time, thinking I should go back soon, because he'd be finished cleaning. But I was pretty shook up by then. I stopped at this place I know and had a couple of quick drinks. Then I went back to the grocery store."

"And?"

"I parked a block away and walked. Sneaked, really, because I didn't know what was going on and … well, okay, I was scared."

He stopped; Cowboy and I out-waited him.

"There were two cars in the parking lot," Cannon said. "And two men. One guy handed the other one a briefcase. After the first one left, the second one looked into the case; then he left, too. I figured that briefcase was full of money."

"Go over the part where you made your brilliant deductions," I said. "I get a big kick out of that part. Tell me again."

Cannon looked wary as he said, "Well, the first guy had to be Carl; that made sense because he had the money to start with. And then I realized why the door was locked; the old guy wasn't cleaning; he really had been killed. And the second guy—that was you, but I didn't know it was you at the time—the second guy had, uh, well, you say you didn't kill him, either, but I thought you had. At the time I thought that. I know better now because you told me, but then, not knowing, I thought you'd done it."

Cannon looked at me to see if he should protest my innocence a few more times, then seemed to decide it wasn't necessary. "When you left, I saw your license number. I was pretty mad because you had my money."

"This time around, I have to ask," I said. "If you didn't kill Max, what made you think you deserved the money?"

"Well, I didn't deserve it, I guess. But I had never intended to kill him, not even in the beginning, and I was always going to take the money. So what was the difference?"

How do you argue with logic like that? "Go on," I said.

"Maybe I didn't work it all out quite that fast, I'm not sure now. I was going to go into the store, I remember that, to see about Max. If he was really dead, I mean. I didn't, though, because right after you left, a car full of cops came. Plainclothes cops, but it was pretty obvious what they were. I hid in an alley across the street and watched for a while. When an ambulance came, that's when I put it all together, I guess. I knew for sure Max was dead then. And you had my money."

"How did you find me?"

"Well, I had your license number, remember. And there's this guy, in the bar I told you about? He's got a buddy who's a cop, so he can find out things like that. It cost me twenty bucks."

I wondered who got the twenty, and if the cop was a rookie trying too hard to impress a civilian, or an old-timer who'd missed out on a promotion he thought he deserved. The rookie wouldn't even know about the twenty; the old-timer would have gotten at least fifteen of it. Whoever it was, they were playing Russian roulette with Internal Affairs.

"Anyway," Cannon said, "with what he found out for me, I knew where you were. I called you a couple of times, but well, talking to you was even goofier than talking to that guy Carl. No offense, but …"

"Don't stroke me, Bert. Just tell your story."

If it is possible for a naked, psyched-out, kidnap-and-inter-rogation victim to appear even more uncomfortable, Cannon did. He squirmed and avoided my eye and bounced his foot and finally said cautiously, "Look, I'm really sorry about the Molotov cocktail. But it was safe; it couldn't explode or anything like that. I would never throw a real one, one with gasoline in it. You got to believe that. I only wanted to scare you, to get you to hand over the money." He squirmed some more and folded his arms. Then he realized that his crotch was exposed. He tried to fold his arms in such a way that he could still keep his hands in his lap, but that didn't work.

I said, "Every time you called, I offered to give you back the money. Why wouldn't you meet me?"

Cannon's face screwed up. He looked ready to cry. "I don't know. Part of the time I thought you were too eager, and it would be a trap. And part of the time I couldn't think of a safe place to meet. And even when I decided on a place and I really wanted to go there, I ... it was ... I was so goddamned *scared!*" He dropped his chin onto his chest. "So I decided to forget the whole thing. Then you guys ... in the coffee shop, you grabbed me and ..." Cannon's shoulders jerked spasmod-ically; tears began to drip on his lowered hands.

Cowboy looked at me over Cannon's bowed head. He shrugged.

I went into the living room and found Tony Cordington's phone number in the mess left over from our search for Bert Cannon. She was home.

"Bert needs help," I said. "Are you still interested enough to give it to him?"

"What kind of help?"

"We had to jolt him pretty good, Tony. He's off the mercenary kick now. Maybe you can keep him off it, maybe not. It'll be up to you two."

"What about the police?" she said. "After you left. I got to thinking about it, and I thought—"

"I was wrong. Bert didn't kill Max Krandorff."

37

"Tony showed up about thirty minutes later," I said to Hilda's open bathroom door, "and took Cannon home with her. She might make it work. I have no idea what the odds are. Fifty-fifty, maybe."

Hilda stuck her head around the door frame. She dried her hair with a big yellow towel that flapped around her face and muffled her voice. "Thupper man."

"'The poor man?' Hey, this is the guy who threw a fire-bomb at you."

"I know, but ..." She stopped drying and stood with the towel draped around her neck, her black curls tangled, her skin pink and fresh from the shower.

"Perhaps you'd care to step over here," I said, "to, ah, facilitate further discussion."

"Relax, big fella. All in good time." She moved out of my sight line from the bed. Her hair dryer began to whir. She called out out over the noise, "Seriously, did you have to torture him like that?"

"You make it sound like rubber hoses and cattle prods to

the gonads. We only psyched him out. He'd have gotten the same treatment being processed into any slammer."

"Taking away his clothes? Treating him like a thing instead of a person?"

"Well, I didn't have time to mess around, so maybe he did get a slightly concentrated dose. Still, it was only basic technique. Take away a man's pants, it loosens his tongue. Same with pretending he's a side of beef. As soon as he knows you have control over him, he'll roll over and try to please you."

Hilda's head again, with halfway-dry hair. "Is that the reaction they call the Stockholm syndrome?"

"A close cousin. Mostly it's just a way you get people to give you what you want."

Hilda disappeared again. "It's not very nice, whatever you call it."

"It's not very nice to agree to kill people or throw firebombs, either. Maybe we broke him of those unsociable habits. By the way, Hil, I've always considered damp hair to be very sexy. Don't go to a lot of trouble in there."

"Relax, it's worth waiting for. You're absolutely certain he didn't kill that man Max at the grocery store."

"Yeah. Cannon's a wannabee, in the first place. Oh, maybe he could kill someone if he concentrated real hard, but I doubt it. The thing is, though, I heard him when he banged on the door that night. I was sitting on the floor next to Max's body at the time."

"Maybe that wasn't him."

"Had to be him," I said. "He wouldn't know that someone else had come to the door, for one thing, and for another, he mentioned the Closed sign I taped to the glass. He's clean."

The hair dryer stopped. "Are you going to tell your police friends about him?" Soft clinks and rustles drifted out the bathroom door.

"I'm still working on that one. I should let Ed Durkee know, but this is a bad time for Bert to be hassled by the cops."

"How considerate of you," Hilda said. "It was all right for you and Cowboy to hassle him, but the police shouldn't?"

"Yes, because we got there first. Cannon thought he was rough and tough, a hotshot mercenary soldier, but he melted down to jelly in less than a day. Now he's pliable. Tony Cordington might turn him around, help him get his life straightened out. But if he was leaned on again too soon, he might crack completely. Or turn paranoid and resentful. Or worse."

"Perhaps," Hilda called.

I said, "But you have a say in it, too, Hil. That firebomb was assault, no matter how you slice it."

"He sounds harmless now. Forget it."

"Okay." I got up and went to the bedroom door, opened it and closed it, twice, hard.

"What was that?" Hilda called.

"Me," I said. "Just slamming it in the door to calm myself down a little bit. This waiting is tough on a guy."

"Ho-ho," she said. A wisp of filmy white material flickered out of the bathroom doorway and immediately withdrew. "You don't know how lucky you are, bucko. This little number is going to curl your toes."

"Am I likely to roar and bellow and paw the carpet like a lust-ravaged beast?"

"Almost certainly," she said. "It's a good thing Cowboy and Mimi went home."

"This sounds promising," I said. "When? When?"

"Soon, soon. Trust me, you're going to love this."

She was right.

38

onday mornings are bad enough under normal conditions. Start of the work week and all that. But most weeks, at least you have an idea what you're trying to accomplish. Finalize the Frobisher contract, paint the Jones house, make more widgets, sell another thousand hamburgers, whatever.

It's harder to face a Monday morning when you don't know where you're going, what you're doing, or what to try next. Not that it matters much, because nothing seems to work.

I went to the office, mostly from force of habit. I picked up a sack of doughnuts on the way and shared them with Beth Woodland in her office on the other side of the big plate glass window. Beth was fine; there was nothing new or strange going on around the building, except for a noon party at the P.R. Guy's office that had ended with the P.R. guy—I can never remember his name—being locked out in the hall in his underwear. "Maybe that's what they mean by public relations," Beth said. "And I got your mail. Here."

By ten o'clock, I had reduced the mail to its component

parts; bills (eight), circulars and other junk (six), and check (one, small, possibly rubber).

At ten-ten, I took Ed Durkee's portable phone back to him. He looked at it glumly. "The Cannon guy wasn't the one, huh?"

"I'm powerless against such relentless interrogation. Cannon was the one, but there's more to it than I thought. Listen to this and tell me what I missed. *Please* tell me what I missed."

I recited The Life and Times of Bert Cannon, a tragedy in three acts. When I finished, Ed dry-scrubbed his face and said, "Aw, hell, I think you're right, Rafferty."

"Thanks a lot."

"I'm gonna pretend I never heard of Cannon," Ed sad. "Why screw him up any more?"

"Do me another favor, Ed. Tell me the Houston cops have found Dresden. Tell me he's confessed to everything from original sin to sabotaging the Titanic."

Ed shrugged. "Sorry."

After a while, I said, "Well, the loose end is annoying, but it's your problem, I guess. I just wanted to find out who threw the firebomb and stop him from doing it again. I guess I did that much."

"Sounds like it," Ed said.

"You guys can work on the murder part of it," I said. "You have the manpower for it. Gotta find Dresden first, anyway."

"Probably," Ed said. "Don't worry about it. Once Kevin Noonebury finishes farting around with the case, I'll see what I can do."

"Ole Kev still flailing away with the bright burning sword of righteousness, is he?"

"Is he ever. Slowing down a little, though. They're starting to pull some of his people away, into other operations. I hear he had to drop some of his surveillance targets. But Kevin's a long way from finished. His MacTuff bandwagon still has all its wheels."

We sat there quietly for a few minutes; then I said, "He'll screw it up if we let him, won't he?"

Ed nodded. "I think so."

"You gonna let him do that, Ed?"

"No."

"Me neither."

———

I went for a drive that afternoon, around and around the parking lots at D-FW airport, in search of a particular light-green Dodge Dynasty. It was Carl Dresden's car, Ed said, and as far as he knew, it had not been seen since Dresden left for Houston. Ergo, ipso, facto, and what the hell, the Dodge might be parked at the airport. And it might be loaded with no end of juicy clues.

Of course it might not be parked at the airport, but even that would tell us something. Either way, checking D-FW for the Dynasty was a job that needed doing.

Idling up and down the lanes in airport parking lots is hard on the butt and the back. The body temperature, too. That Monday wasn't as hot as the day I'd first met Dresden, but it was hot enough. This time I was ready for it, with a cooler of ice and six-pack of beer. Be prepared. And to think the same preparations had gotten me kicked out of Boy Scouts all those years ago

I found the Dynasty. It took from twelve-thirty until four thirty-seven; it took all the beer and most of the ice; it sunburned the hell out of my left arm, but I found that sucker.

And I got it open, too, with the pistol key gadget I'd

borrowed from Don Sweetham, a finance guy who occasionally gets me to repo cars for him.

This did not mean my luck had changed. Because after I'd found the Dynasty, and after I'd opened it up but before I'd searched it, one other thing happened.

I got arrested.

39

"What the hell did you think you were doing?" Noonebury hissed. "You destroyed my surveillance team's cover."

We were back in Noonebury's conference room, at the same blond table. Outside the glass door, Ernie the DEA man strutted around and gloated. In here, Kevin was flanked by the two cops who'd nailed me. They'd been hiding in a Toyota van parked nose to nose with the Dynasty. When they'd boiled out of the van, they surprised the hell out of me. It was a good bust.

When I told them that, Noonebury had become very tight round the eyes. So I told them again.

"In possession of burglary tools, too," Noonebury said. "You may lose your PI license over this."

"Burglary tools, my butt. I was doing a repo. So I got the wrong car, maybe. So what?" I smiled at him. "Do you find yourself becoming forgetful as you get older, too?"

Kevin had his lips pressed too tightly to show me his perfect teeth. "You are not amusing," he said. "You are pathetic. You've been caught in the act of felony auto theft

—as a minimum—and all you can do is make wisecracks."

"Kevin, old buddy, let's think about the good points and the bad points of busting me." One of the young stakeout cops suddenly perked up and looked so damned crimebuster, it was a shame to break his bubble.

I said, "Relax, kid. I'm not going to offer him a bribe. I'm talking about the political considerations."

Kevin squared his shoulders and said haughtily, "I do not deal in political considerations."

"Uh-huh," I said, and put my feet on his pretty table.

The eager cop stood up, ready to slap my feet away, but Noonebury said, "Um, wait a minute, Jenkinson. Let's, er …" They all went to stand by the door and buzz at each other. Noonebury patted their shoulders and nodded paternally and eventually the stakeout cops went outside. Noonebury returned to the table and sat down. I noticed for the first time he had faint bags under his eyes.

"You gotta get more sleep, Kevin. Baggy eyes look terrible on the tube."

"What political considerations?" he said. "Don't waste my time."

"If you try to roust me with a bullshit felony-auto-theft rap, I'll go public with the whole Dresden fiasco."

"That won't do you any good, Rafferty," Kevin said. He stood up. "Really, that is—"

"I found the guy who Dresden hired to whack his partner. Your two-bit task force couldn't find him, but I did. You want the chief to read all about it over his morning cornflakes?"

"Give me whatever you have," Noonebury said. "You are required to cooperate with a police investigation." He was frowning now, no longer the steadfast police administrator. But not political. Oh, no.

"There are conditions," I said. "First, I won't tell you who the man is, because, the way it turned out, he didn't do it. Second, in addition to forgetting this, er, misunderstanding, you keep your people off my back when I go to Dresden's office tomorrow. Third, get Ed Durkee up here. I want to talk to him first."

Noonebury's cheeks turned pink, and his right hand quivered. By his standards the man was gripped by uncontrollable fury. "Never! You cannot demand—"

"Okay. Lock me up. A month from now, look around and see who got hurt the most."

Noonebury sputtered and spat, then he went away to talk to a handful of his people. I smiled and waved to them. Thirty minutes later, Ed Durkee ambled into the conference room. He closed the door behind him and lowered himself into a chair like a brown balloon deflating. "I hear you found the Dodge," he said. "And ruined Kevin's day."

I told him what I'd said to Noonebury so far and what I proposed to say.

"Should work," Ed said. "Leave out Cannon's name if you want." Ed shrugged. He looked bored.

I said, "It means changing the story I told him before. Slightly."

"Don't worry about it. Kevin's pretty sure you were in the store a lot longer than you'd said, anyway."

"Is he likely to renege and try to bust me anyway?"

Ed grinned. "Kevin won't renege. He'd look sneaky and untrustworthy if he did. He couldn't stand that."

And that's the way it went down. Noonebury listened carefully, frowned a lot—mostly at me but part of the time at Ed—and finally, when I had finished, he got up and walked toward the conference room door.

"Kevin," Ed said, "considering all this, how about dropping this one back into my basket? It's obvious this isn't a crack case."

Kevin Noonebury stood facing the glass panel, looking out at his evening-shift minions. They had pulled in another street kid. This kid was older and meaner looking than the first one but he didn't seem to be answering Frigerio's questions, either.

Noonebury sucked in a lungful of air and let it out noisily. It was a strange gesture for him. "No, Ed," he said. "This *is* a drug case. You'll see that in the end." He opened the door and walked out.

"Hey, wait," I yelled at his back. "What about the Dodge? Let's toss the Dodge."

Noonebury kept going across the big room and entered a small office on the far side.

Ed looked at me with his sleepy face. "Forget it. On the way up here I found out they tossed the Dodge three days ago, when they found it."

"And?"

"And there was nothing useful in it," Ed said. "Not a single goddamned thing. Ain't that a bitch?"

————

"How many sandwiches for you?" Hilda said.

"Three, if there's enough ham. Thanks."

I'd come to Hilda's house at eight-thirty, annoyed at having wasted the entire day messing around with Dresden's car and Noonebury's ego. Hilda had already eaten, but she offered to fix me a snack while I drank a beer, read the paper, and calmed down.

Reading the paper didn't calm me down any.

"You ought to see this book review, Hil," I said. "It's

enough to make you sick. This Englishman named, uh, Robert Lawrence, wrote a book about the Falkland Islands war. He was, let me see, a Scots Guard lieutenant, whatever that is. Platoon commander, it says. Anyway, Lawrence was wounded and not expected to live, but he did, and he got a medal and he wrote this book."

Hilda sliced ham and said, "Okay. So?"

"So this silly-ass book reviewer doesn't bother to review the book; he just takes potshots at Lawrence and Maggie Thatcher and the military in general. He is, quote, troubled by the adolescent glorification of brutal conflict, end quote. According to him war is barbaric and subhuman. Probably carcinogenic, too."

"A lot of people don't like fighting, Rafferty."

"That's not the point. Lawrence was a soldier. He had a job to do. He did it. Where does this numbnuts reviewer get off bad-mouthing him for that?"

Hilda piled ham slices and cheese onto bread. "You are testy tonight, aren't you?"

"This guy doesn't understand," I said. "This wimp's never risked anything. His biggest worry is that he won't get a good stool at the sushi bar."

"Now you sound like one of those magazine ads you told me about. Rafferty-bo, the mercenary wannabee."

"Hil, I understand how those guys feel. Some of them are turkeys, sure, but some of them have been there. They know what it's like to put your butt on the line for something, to feel alive and sharp on top of a bad situation. They want to feel like that again."

Hilda slashed through the sandwiches and dumped them onto a plate. "Men!"

"Damn right. Not like this wimp."

40

Tuesday morning I went to the Mini-Maxi Food Barn office. Sharon Palmerston, the woman I'd phoned a week ago, was alone at the reins of the bustling corporate headquarters.

Well, maybe bustling wasn't quite the word.

There were three desks in a single office, and what looked to be a small storage-coffee-junk room in the back.

All three desks were untidy, in a comfortable, getting-the-work-done sort of way. Two of the desk chairs were empty, Sharon Palmerston sat in the third.

Her desk sign told me that; she didn't. She was sound asleep.

I cleared my throat, and her head came sluggishly up from her desktop.

She was a round-faced blonde in her early thirties, large framed, and her eyes were dull with fatigue. She blinked and absently dragged her fingers through her hair. "Uh, I'm so sorry. I must have … May I help you?"

"No problem. Late night?" I showed her one of my more charming smiles, to go with my relaxed, easygoing nature.

She nodded and yawned behind her hand. "I'll say. It was after midnight before I finished the payroll; then I had to take the checks to all the stores and … Who are you? Should I be telling you all this?"

"Absolutely," I said. "Rafferty. I'm investigating Mr. Krandorff's, er …" I hadn't worked out yet exactly which lie to tell her, so I wasn't sure whether to say "homicide" or "reported death" or "unfortunate demise."

"Oh," she said and blinked again. "For the insurance company?"

"That's right. The keyman policy. So, I'd like to ask you a few—"

"Who put in the claim? I haven't seen any paperwork on it, and I've done everything else around here."

I got out my pocket notebook and frowned seriously while I read last week's grocery list. "Well, I do these routine investigations on a contract basis; I'm not from head office or anything like that. But according to my notes, a Mr. Carl Drysdale—"

"Dresden," she said. "Carl Dresden, but—"

"—advised the head office. Ah, through his attorney, apparently. Hmm." I grinned at her sheepishly. "Actually, that may have been his accountant. I didn't quite get …" You foxy devil, Rafferty.

Sharon nodded and seemed relieved. "Oh, right," She said. "That makes sense, then. Neville Compton—he's our accountant—has been a lot of help since … since this horrible mess started."

"Good," I said. "Now, is Mr. Dresden in?"

"Well, no, he's not," Sharon said. She straightened her desk blotter and shifted a paperweight an inch to the left, then moved it back to its original position. "He's out of town on business."

"Uh-oh," I said.

"Is that a problem?" She was defensive now.

"Well ..."

"Mr. Rafferty, believe me, I can tell you anything you need to know. I've been with Mini-Maxi for years. Even Mr. Dresden says they couldn't get along without me. That sounds immodest, but it's true." She set her jaw and nodded, so there.

"Now that you mention it," I said, "it might be easier this way. Because claims on a keyman policy can be so sensitive." I had drifted into a whiny kind of persona I didn't like very much, but it seemed to be working. Not easy, this racket.

I stopped talking and tried for a reluctant, concerned look. Eventually Sharon prompted me with, "Sensitive in what way?"

"Well, the questions I have to ask. They sound like I don't believe what happened, like I'm trying to trap someone. Which is not true, not at all. I get paid to make a report and, let's face it, we all have our little hoops to jump through, don't we?"

"Of course," Sharon said. "I understand how you feel."

She smiled and motioned me toward a chair at the nearest desk. I sat down and smiled back. Talk to me, I said with my eyes. Tell me everything you know about this wacky outfit.

She did.

Over the next hour Sharon told me how Dresden had started with a single store ten years ago. Max Krandorff was a relative newcomer; he came in as a partner four years back. Almost immediately Mini-Maxi Food Barns took off. Krandorff was a street-shrewd wheeler-dealer; Dresden was good with boring but critical things like state licenses and reports, taxes, insurance plans, and employee-training programs. The way Sharon Palmerston told it, Carl and Max were perfect candidates for a keyman policy. They were dynamite together, but either one alone would need a miracle to keep the business afloat.

"Not that things have been easy," Sharon said. "Especially with Number Three." She sighed. "I feel so sorry for them. Number Three looked so good on paper, and it was so important that it do well, but believe me, *everything* has gone wrong with that location. The latest problem is kids."

"Shoplifting?" I said. "Vandalism?"

"No, no. Oh, some of that goes on everywhere, but Number Three's no worse than the others. The thing is, these kids started hanging around the store. Really hoody kids, you know? Mean-looking. And they drove customers away."

"Didn't the police help?"

"Well, they didn't *drive* people away, like poking knives at them; I didn't mean that. It's just, well, women won't go into a store with a *gang* out front, will they?" There was a touch of Valley Girl in her tone and grimace when she said *gang*. Well, gag me with a switchblade.

I said, "Why was the third store so important?"

Sharon leaned confidentially across the gap between the desks. "I'm not sure of the details, but I think Mr. Krandorff had talked Mr. Dresden into expanding too fast. They used to fight a lot about the loan payments. Mr. Dresden said, what with property values slipping, they'd overcapitalized the site. He said the asset value was below the indebtedness. Cash flow was down too. Once, we had to slip the payables back two weeks. And darn it, just when things looked better at Number Three, those rotten kids—oh, my God, listen to me. Hey, when I said *fight*, I didn't mean … Mr. Dresden and Mr. Krandorff argued, that's all. A little bit. Everybody *argues* sometimes."

"I understand, Sharon." I smacked my lips and said, "Is there a coffee shop around here anywhere?"

She jumped up immediately. "Oh, no, no. I'll make some." Over her shoulder, while heading for the back room, she said, "How do you take it?"

"Black."

"Only be a minute," she called from out of sight.

Rafferty's Rule Twenty-nine: Don't steal evidence in front of witnesses.

The empty desk, the one neither of us was using, had to be Dresden's. There was a picture of Dresden's wife beside the blotter. And there was also a big office diary there, too. I grabbed the diary, opened the front door, and threw the diary into the front seat of the Mustang parked out front.

I was sitting down again, smiling vaguely, when Sharon poked her head out of the back room and said, "Ready in a second."

"Thank you."

She went away again, but I didn't have time to do much more than paw through Max's desk drawers. There didn't seem to be anything important, though I didn't have enough time to be certain. I might have to burgle this place yet.

Then Sharon was back with two steaming mugs of coffee and more of the Mini-Maxi saga.

Max Krandorff was a bachelor and a wonderful man; Carl Dresden was a wonderful man, too, but, you know, kind of vanilla; had I met Mrs. Dresden yet, and wasn't she simply the nicest lady ever?

I said, "It must have been a shock when Mr. Krandorff was—"

"Please," she said, shaking her head rapidly. "Let's not talk about that. It's too … I don't believe it yet. I—" She bit her lower lip and waved vaguely at the paperwork crowding her desk. "—I don't have time to cry now. There's so much to do."

"One more thing," I said. "About Mr. Dresden. Doesn't it seem strange to you that he hasn't come back yet?"

Sharon started to speak, but her lip quivered too much. She bit down on it for several seconds, then said, "I'm worried sick about that. He must be ill, or maybe he was in an accident, or who knows what. Why, he could be in a hospital unconscious and we wouldn't know!"

"If you like, I could speak to some of my friends on the police force about that," I said, and immediately wished I hadn't. It wasn't necessary to con her about sensitive things like that. Sometimes I go too far.

"Oh, thank you. That would be very kind." She seemed genuinely grateful.

I left after that, dragging my tattered self-respect along behind me. Sharon shakily smiled good-bye from her desk and dived into a pile of wholesale grocery invoices. I decided if I ever needed a secretary, I'd try to steal Sharon from Mini-Maxi.

I drove across the street and pulled into the drive-in two slots down from the MacTuff cop still gallantly watching the Mini-Maxi office. I grinned at them and waved. They glowered at me and kept glowering while I drank coffee and flipped through Carl Dresden's desk diary.

Isn't it depressing to see public servants with an attitude problem?

41

resden's diary was a large one, with a full page for each day, plus all the usual crap in the front that tells you the summer temperature range in Vladivostok and what time it is in Dubai.

Leafing through the diary, I didn't expect to find a notation like "11:30—hire Joe Jones to kill Max," though that would have been nice. The nearest thing to it was Tony Cordington's phone number on the page for the day before Dresden had phoned her apartment looking for Eagle.

Dresden also used his diary as a scratch pad; if he hadn't filled a page with things-to-do-that-day, he went back and used the blank space for odd notes and calculations and doodles. Not every past page was that way, but many were. There was no order to them, not that I could see. Apparently he just flipped back to an empty spot and scribbled away.

There were several such pages crammed with figures, vaguely similar to the calculations we'd found in his house. Again, his personal shorthand made them difficult to interpret, but I began to think the numbers were units of thousands; they concerned the business; and they were attempts to figure the way out of a bad cash-flow period. Part of that feeling came from the only obviously identifiable calculation in the diary. That entry worked out the difference in monthly loan payments if the principal amount was suddenly reduced by three hundred thousand dollars.

I bet myself I now knew the face value of Mini-Maxi's keyman insurance policy.

But aside from that, the diary left me with more questions than answers. Questions like: Had Dresden hired someone *other* than Bert Cannon to hit Max? If so, who? And if so, why did he keep Bert—and me, because of his confusion about us —on the string? And why did he pay me? Aside from because he thought I was Bert.

From there the questions became even hairier. If Dresden didn't hire someone else, then who killed Max? Could it have been a real robbery that simply happened at a time and place where it had confused everyone? Or was there a thrill-killer somewhere chuckling over the fun he'd had listening to Max plead for his life?

Or was the answer something entirely different, something I had missed all along? Or hadn't thought of yet?

How bewildered could I get? Step closer, my friends. See Rafferty think so hard, his brains melt and run out his ears. Getcha tickets here …

Hell with it. I gave up before I hurt myself and went looking for a phone book. A pay phone two blocks north had the front half of the business pages still intact and, yes, Neville Compton, CPA, would see me in thirty minutes.

So I drove to the Lemmon Avenue address Compton's secretary gave me, not so much because I honestly thought I would learn much, but because everyone has to be somewhere.

———

Neville Compton was round. He wasn't fat, not grossly so. He was only plump, with round pale eyes and round spectacles and a bowling ball skull and rounded shoulders and a button nose and a small, round mouth. He was an amalgamation of circular shapes, and he was also perhaps the calmest man I have ever met.

"I'm truly sorry, Mr. Rafferty," he said, "but I cannot divulge details of my clients' business dealings." He spoke slowly and smiled apologetically and seemed to be saying that if it were up to him, why, certainly …

"The problem is," I said, "that half the Dallas police department is working overtime to prove your clients—and maybe you, for all I know—are drug dealers. I'm trying to stop that. Well, not specifically to stop it, but the effect will be the same. You really should help me."

"How extraordinary," Compton said without raising his voice. "Why don't you tell me about it?"

I told him. I left out the part about Dresden wanting to kill Max, and I exaggerated Kevin Noonebury's ability to prove a drug case, and I implied I was working for a secret DPD investigative group. But I told him enough of the truth to make it sound logical. What the hell, it's an imperfect world.

When I'd finished, Neville Compton said, "Amazing," the way anyone else would say, "More coffee?"

"Now it's your turn," I said. "And I'm prepared to deny I've ever been here."

"Yes, I think that would be wise. Well, well, where shall begin?" He leaned back in his chair and propped his elbows on the arms of his chair. His fingers met in a steeple shape in front of his face and ruined his round look. I felt like telling him to do something else with his hands.

Compton said, "I see the problem, of course. And, like Sharon, I am concerned about Carl's long stay in Houston. I trust he is well. Forgive me, I digress. Now then, Carl and Max are—or were, which is perhaps the appropriate word at this juncture—quite different people. I've always seen Max as the quintessential trader. Sometimes a profane man, often crude, but shrewd and exceedingly numerate. Not in the sense of formal accounting, of course. He even claimed to be baffled by double-entry bookkeeping, though I believe that was an affectation.

"Max knew about business. He knew how to buy and how to sell, and he knew his profit to the last half cent per unit." Compton beamed fondly. "I like to think of Max as a Viking. The Norse were actually traders and merchants, you know. That bloodthirsty Viking-raiding-party image is largely made up."

"What about Dresden?" I said. Vikings, schmikings.

"Carl is, as I say, very different. He's quite a nervous man. Meticulous in his approach to business, which is, I believe, a way to assuage his personal anxieties. Carl is a conservative man; it goes without saying. He is often fearful of the, oh, call it the swashbuckling attitude toward business that Max preferred."

Compton sat and smiled gently to himself. He was so relaxed and peaceful, he might have been an old man rocking on a sunny porch, daydreaming about his grandchildren. "Two intriguing men," he said, "who complemented each other nicely. A good business team."

"I gather there were problems with the third store."

He nodded slowly. "Yes. That was an unfortunate location, I believe. Max insisted it would be profitable, but he may have been mistaken. Perhaps on that occasion Max sank his own longboat, to use a Viking analogy.

"At any rate, there was a squabble about the third store. Carl didn't like the location; Max insisted. Carl finally acquiesced, but by opening time, the project was grossly over budget. Max ordered new signs for all three stores, for one thing, and there were delivery delays on, um, the roof trusses, I believe. And at the best of times, the Mini-Maxi Food Barn standard building represents a sizable capital expenditure. The buildings are distinctive, they draw a great deal of traffic, they win awards, but on a square-footage basis ..." Compton shuddered gently.

"But forgive me," he said, "It is not my place to criticize such things. The significant fact is, the third store opened much further in the red than budgeted. And the first-quarter trading losses were very bad. Recently Max said he expected a new scheme to recoup those losses. I believe it was to be a grand marketing ploy, though I have no idea of the details. It would have been imaginative, I'm sure. It was certainly needed. That location, for some reason, attracted a rather, ah, unfortunate class of young customer. The young people spent very little but their presence degraded the ambience."

Compton shrugged slowly. "Whatever Max had in mind, it's too late now. He's gone. Marketing is not, I fear, Carl's forte. I doubt very much if that store can ever trade its way into the black."

"I don't understand these things," I said. "How bad is that? Are we talking about closing the store or no year-end bonuses for the staff or what?"

"Closing the store would shave the monthly operating, but it would also cut gross sales for the chain." He frowned. "And there are certain long-term agreements with suppliers. Also, the building construction, fittings, and advertising costs are all liabilities incurred long ago. They won't disappear from the books. There has already been one refinancing. The bank may approve another, but it would certainly insist on operational restrictions."

Compton thought about it, then said, "I would say the entire Mini-Maxi operation—that is, all three stores—is less than two months from Chapter 11."

"Chapter ...?"

"Oh, sorry," he said. "Bankruptcy."

42

left Compton's office at one-thirty and went to Houston.

Not directly to Houston, exactly. First I went to the cop shop and talked to Ed Durkee. When I told him what I had in mind he gave me a photo of Carl Dresden. He wouldn't tell where he got it.

"Look out, Kevin Noonebury," I said. "The brown bombshell is on the move."

"Get out of here," Ed growled. "But keep in touch."

Next I went to Gardner's Antiques. Hilda was behind the desk, doing boss-lady things. "Tell you what," I said, "if a good-looking broad took the rest of the day off, she could be my main squeeze on a trip to Houston."

She put down her pen and thought about it. "More information," she said.

"Jet to Houston with a handsome dude at your side. Stay at the Holiday Inn with a handsome dude at your side. Shop at the Galleria while the handsome—"

"Sold!" Hilda said.

By the time we packed, got to the airport, caught a Southwest shuttle and cabbed to the Holiday Inn, it was almost six before I started showing Dresden's picture to Holiday Inn desk clerks.

"Excuse me for a moment, sir," the second one said. "I'll just double check with the assistant manager." Which meant I got shuffled off to the hotel security people. We killed another forty-five minutes establishing I was me, not a blackmailer or hotel burglar looking for a fat mark.

Eventually they were won over by my sterling personality and began to tell me things. There was one desk clerk who had checked Dresden in—"Completely normal check-in, American Express card, one bag, I think, and an open-ended room requirement. Did I do something wrong?"—and a telephone operator who remembered him calling a few times for messages.

"Where he called from, I have no idea," she said. "It's not unusual for people to check for messages by phone."

Aside from those two, there was general agreement that Dresden showed, shall we say, a minimal use of hotel facilities. "Can we toss his room?" I said to the security guy, a tall redhead named Gurley.

Gurley looked like his stomach hurt. "No. You can knock on the door, but if he's not there, I won't let you in."

"Don't bother to come up with me," I said. "I can find it."

"I'm sure you could," Gurley said. "I'll come up anyway."

So we knocked, looked at the door of 1417 for a few minutes, then rode the elevator back down to the lobby. "You might talk to the morning shift," Gurley said. "I'll tell Brownlow, my relief, to expect you. See him first, okay?"

———

The next morning Hilda departed for the Galleria with shopping fervor bright in her eye. I found Brownlow. He was shorter than Gurley, with a salt-and-pepper crew cut and a perpetual smile.

"How can I help you?" he said. "Come on, let's see if we can help you today."

We went back over the same ground I'd covered with Gurley. The desk people didn't recognize Dresden's photo. Neither did the bell captain, the bell staff, the parking garage attendants, anyone from the restaurant or bars, the staff … trust me, no one.

Brownlow said, "I know the cleaning staff keeps sending memos asking if 1417 is really occupied, because it's never used." His smile turned apologetic. "I don't know what else I can do for you."

"Don't sweat it. Thanks."

Brownlow went back to more normal work, and I shuffled off to drink lunch. I hadn't expected to suddenly solve the Dresden disappearance overnight; I knew I was going back over ground the Houston PD had already covered, but even so …

Halfway through my third beer, I noticed a waitress pointing me out to a young woman in a blue suit and frilly blouse. I could imagine the conversation: *That's him. Hotshot from Dallas who thinks he can — "*

"Mr. Rafferty?" the woman in blue said. "There's a phone call for you. A police officer in Dallas. I thought it might be important."

———

"Ed said I was to tell you," Sergeant Ricco rasped. "We found Dresden. You can stop playing with yourself down there."

"Dresden's in Dallas?" I said. "But—"

"Naw, he ain't here, but he ain't in Houston, either. We

don't know yet if he's been hiding in Galveston all along, but that's where they found him this morning."

"Galveston," I said.

"Yeah. I gotta go now. Ed says call him when you get back in town."

"Hey, wait a minute, Ricco! What does Dresden say? Why did Galveston pick him up?"

Ricco cackled down the phone line. "Say? He ain't talking. And Galveston picked him up because his body was floating in the goddamned ship channel."

43

Hilda came back to the hotel at noon, alternately bubbly over her shopping triumphs and moaning about her sore feet. I had already packed most of our clothes and checked the departure time of every flight to Dallas that afternoon.

We squeaked onto a one-fifteen that was running late or was a special or something. Whatever it was, the door didn't quite hit us in the backside getting on but almost. After takeoff I squirmed, wondered why they were flying the thing so goddamned slow, and muttered to myself.

Hilda, wisely, napped.

In Dallas I dropped Hilda at her house and drove downtown to police headquarters. I hit Ed Durkee's office door with a dozen questions in mind. "Ed, what the hell is—"

"Here," he said, and handed me the receiver of that portable phone on the floor beside his desk. "It's for you. I forgot to have that call splitter changed. Sorry."

"Oh, for Christ's sa—hello!"

The voice on the phone was almost a caricature of a

Hispanic accent. "Eh, Rafferty, joo gonna geeve me dat money? Or you want to go sweeming like your *amigo* Dresden?"

"You can have the money," I said. "Why don't you pick it up in an hour?"

44

I t wasn't quite an hour, more like fifty-five minutes later when a new black Buick Electra ghosted to a stop in front of my house. There were several people in it.

I hadn't been home for more than ten minutes, and I was still keyed up. It wasn't easy to sit down in the living room armchair and wait for them to come in.

They didn't knock. The front door suddenly flew open and banged against the wall. The knob went through the sheetrock.

"Eh, Rafferty-man, how joo doing?" The first one to come through the door was eighteen, maybe, give or take a year. His hair was slicked back with grease. His three-piece gray tailored suit had to be a thousand-dollar item. He had a pencil mustache and a fresh manicure and manic eyes. He was probably no more life-threatening than a blind airline pilot.

He swaggered into my living room and looked around. "Man, dis is a dump! Why joo wanna live in a dump like this, ennyway?"

Behind him, three other Hispanic youths slipped into the room. They wore designer jeans and baggy shirts, up-market, but not straight from the set of Wall Street like their main man. All three backup boys were armed. A weedy-one with a straggly goatee carried an Uzi; the other two had oversize handguns.

The showboat in the suit suddenly spread his arms wide and said, "Eh, where's my manners? So sorry, Rafferty-man, I dint introduce myself. Call me Hector." He pronounced it Hec —*tor*." These are my, ah, bizniz associates, awright?"

Hector's "bizniz associates" stared at me with varying looks on their faces. The most pleasant expression was mild disgust.

I nodded at them and waited. It was still Hector's move.

"Joo prolly wonderin' what's goin' on, Rafferty-man," Hector said. "Zat right?"

"That's right."

"It's simple, man. A bizniz arrangement fell troo, joo might say. I got ripped off. Imagine dat, rippin' off Hector! Some people, man, dey is too dumb to live."

"Life can be difficult," I said.

"Hey, Diego, joo hear that? Rafferty-man sez life can be difficult. Well, no shit, huh?"

I said, "What I don't understand is why you want this money."

Hector's eyes looked even more freaky. "Why? Why the fuck not, man? Goddamned old *hijo de puta* rips off my crack stash, it costs me money! I want it back."

I patted the attaché case beside my chair. "This isn't your money, Hector. I earned this. I killed Max."

"Bullshit, man, joo din't kill heem! Who joo t'ink joo are, tryin' to tell Hector dat? Goddamned *loco* Anglo. Joo peess me off." He paced two steps, turned, paced back, and said, "Fuck thees! I was gonna be easy with joo, Rafferty-man, but now …" He gestured abruptly to the one with the Uzi. "Diego—"

The Uzi swiveled my way, but it hadn't quite come to bear when Cowboy leaned in the window and shot Diego in the side of the head. I was out of my chair by then, with the .45 from beneath my pant leg in one fist. As I rolled and twisted across the floor, I snapped off a shot at Hector and knew I'd missed as soon as I pulled the trigger.

The noise from the various muzzle blasts was a painful, jolting roar in the small room. Behind that roar, as if from far away, I heard shouted curses laced with fear. That may have been me.

The smallest drug dealer, who couldn't have been more than fifteen, tried very hard to kill me. Avoiding his first two shots, I misjudged the distance and came up short, crammed awkwardly against a wall with my gun hand trapped under my side.

The boy killer giggled and bounced like a boxer as he dragged the big magnum down from over his head, where the massive recoil had kicked it. He was a full second too slow. Mimi stood up behind the sofa and nailed him in the chest with her shotgun.

I think it was Ed Durkee who took out the third gunslinger, from the dining room doorway, shooting from a police-academy-perfect combat crouch.

I don't know who shot Hector, not that it mattered. When the noise stopped and I looked through the haze—who says modern ammunition is smokeless?—I saw Hector crumpled against the side wall, with his chin on his chest and his legs straight out in front of him. His chest bubbled when he breathed. There was a new Beretta near his left hand, but he wasn't reaching for it.

Mimi went around the room, checking the casualties. "One of these isn't too bad," she said. "Busted knee, that's all."

Ed Durkee grunted. "I'll get an ambulance." He pointed

his finger at Cowboy and Mimi. "And you two get out of here! Leave a shotgun, or we'll never sell this to the department, but you two go!" He stalked out of the living room, then returned immediately. "Don't think this changes anything," he growled at Cowboy. "We're not on the same side, and we never will be." He left again, and soon I heard him yelling into the kitchen phone.

Cowboy toed the Beretta away from Hector and waved his shotgun barrel like a pointer. "Sucking chest wound," he said. "This one ain't gonna make it."

Hector groaned and rolled his head sideways. He looked up at me. "Hey, man, joo said joo'd give me dat money."

"I lied," I said. "Sue me."

45

"They killed Bert Cannon, too," I said. "After he told them I was the one with the money."

Hilda wriggled her mouth in disgust. "When?"

"About the time we were leaving Houston, apparently. The only one of the little bastards who survived doesn't know everything but he's telling everything he knows." I checked Hilda's wineglass—still half-full—and opened another beer for myself. "Seeing Hec-*tor* and his other buddies get blown away gave him an acute interest in good citizenship."

It was Friday, two days after the living room firefight. My house still smelled of burned powder; maybe it would forever. Hilda and I were trying to get away from it all with another backyard barbecue and sipping session. But we couldn't get away from the tangled Mini-Maxi screwup; that kept drifting back at us.

"They'd found Dresden in Houston, god only knows how," I said. "He was holed up in one of those scungy dumps on Westheimer, so maybe a junkie turned him in for a pocket full of dreamtime. Anyway, Dresden gave them Tony Cordington's phone number and said that was who he gave the money to. They whacked Dresden and came back to Dallas. Then they found Bert at Tony Cordington's apartment—"

"Is she all right?"

"Yeah. Ed located her in a layover hotel in Tampa."

"Sorry, go ahead."

"Bert told Hector he didn't get the money, but I did, so … there you go." I wiggled farther down in my chair and looked at Hilda. "What makes me feel like a first class jerk is that Noonebury was right all along," I said. "About the Mini-Maxi being a crack stash, anyway. It seems that Max—our quintessential Viking—made a deal with Hector. The Mini-Maxi needed cash flow, and Hector would pay big money for Max to hide crack in the back room. Or wherever he hid it; I don't think they know yet."

Hilda waved her arm at me and twitched her head. "Look over there," she mouthed silently.

The orange cat had moved out of the shrubbery in the corner of the yard and sat watching us. It dropped its head and licked its chest twice, then went back to its imitation of a statue.

"Come here, Cat," I said.

It didn't.

I took the last hamburger patty, the one we hadn't eaten, and put it on the ground by my chair.

"Nobody knows exactly how Max and Hector got together," I said to Hilda, "but they did. And that's why a few kids were always hanging around the store. They were watching the crack. While Noonebury was out busting crack houses in south and west Dallas, Hector was warehousing across town. How 'bout that?"

Hilda shook her head. "But why did they kill Max?"

"The kid canary says—aha!"

The cat trotted a dozen feet closer to me—probably closer to the hamburger patty, really—and sat down again. It took another bath.

"The kid canary says when they went to the store one night to withdraw the evening's sale stock, some of their crack was missing. A lot of crack, I guess. Max wouldn't tell them where it was, so they whacked him. Chopped his hand with a machete, too, and kneecapped him. Sort of a multi-cultural *'See what happens to people who mess with us'* warning."

"But if no one knew Max was connected with ..."

"I said they were mean; I didn't say they were smart."

Hilda said, "Did Dresden know about Max's crack plans?"

I shrugged.

"So we'll never know what Dresden blamed Max for, the business downturn or the drug involvement. But either way, to get the insurance payoff and avoid bankruptcy, Dresden was willing to have Max killed. And at the same time, Max was trying to save the company his way, by going into the drug business with stolen crack." Hilda sipped her wine. "Do I have all that right?"

"A cogent summation, my dear."

"Oh, look, Rafferty. Here, kitty, kitty."

The cat had moved again. Now it was only six feet from the hamburger patty.

"How you doing, Cat?" I said. "Come on over and eat."

The cat yawned a boy-am-I-cool yawn. I'd know one of those yawns anywhere.

After a minute or two, when the cat hadn't come any closer, Hilda said, "Because Noonebury was right about the crack, are you and Ed Durkee in trouble?"

"Us?" I said. "That gallant duo, the two-gun heroes of the morning papers and the evening news? Surely you jest."

Hilda shook her head. "I'll never believe another news story of my life."

"Not a bad philosophy. Food's here, Cat. Come and get it."

The cat waited awhile, so I wouldn't think it was obeying me or anything silly like that, then it walked closer. Now it leaned forward and sniffed at the hamburger still about eighteen inches from its nose.

"Hoo-oo, Muffin!" a woman's voice shrilled somewhere close. "Where are you?"

The cat's head swiveled around so fast it looked like it would twist off. The cat stared at the back fence.

A woman's head appeared over the top of the fence. She had curlers in her hair and a screechy voice. "Oh, there you are, Muffin, you naughty cat."

"Is it yours?" I said.

"I hope so," the woman said. They were pink curlers, with a yellow net shower-cap gadget stretched over them. "Muffin's a stray, I think, but we just moved in and—oh, I don't believe we've met!"

"No, we haven't," I said.

Curlers let that one dangle in the air for a while; then she said, "I've been feeding him, so I guess he's mine now." She smiled and said, "I named him Muffin," as if she was proud of it. "Him loves him's fishie-wishies, don't you, Muffin?"

"Oh, my God," Hilda muttered.

Curlers beamed at all of us, then her head dropped down out of sight.

The cat and I watched her go, then it looked at the hamburger.

"Hey, Cat," I said.

It looked up at me.

"Here's the deal. Over there you may be Muffin with

fishy-whatsits, but over here, you're Cat with cold hamburger. Work it out for yourself."

Hilda said, "Rafferty, you're crazy."

Cat didn't think so. He came over and ate the hamburger. And purred.

— *THE END* —

Rafferty returns in
Fatal Sisters

Her husband's gone. She says he's a spy.
Rafferty thinks he's a con.

Three days missing, and Sherm Akister's already neck-deep
in lies, mob money, and a case that smells worse the closer
Rafferty gets.

Then Sherm turns up dead—and Rafferty finds himself
caught in the middle of a turf war that's about to blow Dallas
wide open.

Tense, gritty, and packed with bite—*Fatal Sisters* pulls no
punches. Scan the QR code below to get your copy.

Read Now

DID YOU ENJOY THIS BOOK?

Reviews and recommendations are the best ways to help another reader have as much fun as you did.

And no matter whether you loved this book or not, I'd appreciate it if you could take the time to leave a review. It can be as short or as long as you like.

Scan to leave your review

And if you do leave a review, I'd love to read it!
Email me the link at **bill@duncanandlee.com**

DUNCAN & LEE

Bill Duncan & Catherine Lee make up the Australian crime-writing duo of Duncan & Lee. They have more ideas than time and their typing speed will ever let them create.

———

DUNCAN & LEE BOOK SERIES

Eden Cross FBI Mysteries

Detective Bonnie Hunter Thrillers

Rafferty P.I. Mysteries

Detective Charlie Cooper Mysteries

Scan the QR code for more information.

ABOUT THE AUTHOR

BILL DUNCAN lives with his wife, Australian crime writer Catherine Lee, in the coastal city of Newcastle, Australia and defines a great day as one spent plotting how to get away with murder and drinking coffee. Always coffee.

He was born in a small town just north of Dallas, Texas before the family immigrated to Australia when he was 7 years old. While he studied Architecture at university, his father wrote a six-book mystery series featuring Rafferty, a Dallas P.I.

In 2017, after 20 years working in the design and construction industry, Bill obtained a rights reversion for the Rafferty books and launched them in ebook format for the first time. He continues to write new Rafferty stories and the growing series has become a hit with over 300,000 readers around the world.

He has no dogs or cats, but two adult children he shamelessly adores, and a vinyl record collection with an unhealthy proportion of 1980's releases.

Get in touch with Bill at: **bill@duncanandlee.com**